FACEOFF

KELLY JAMIESON

AUTHOR NOTE

This story is a Canadian fantasy—a hockey fantasy. For years, it was no secret that two businessmen wanted to purchase an NHL team and bring it back to Winnipeg. Despite years of rumors, disappointments and false reports of done deals, hockey fans in Winnipeg continued to fantasize about the NHL returning.

My first Heller Brothers Hockey book *Breakaway* is the story of Jase Heller, a professional hockey player from Winnipeg who has three brothers. As I worked on edits to *Breakaway*, it seemed these Winnipeg businessmen were very close to purchasing the Phoenix Coyotes (which were the Winnipeg Jets up until 1996). Thinking ahead, I changed the team Tag Heller played for to a (fictional!) team in Phoenix and when I started writing *Faceoff*, Tag's story, I wrote the fantasy—the NHL had returned to Winnipeg!

I had not yet submitted this manuscript to my editor when the real life story changed—it was no longer the Phoenix Coyotes being purchased, it was the Atlanta Thrashers. I couldn't change my story to match reality because I'd already planted the seed that Tag Heller played for Phoenix in *Breakaway*. I named the new Winnipeg team the Jets in my book—at that point we didn't know for sure the deal would even happen and if it did, whether a new

Winnipeg team would be called the Jets or something entirely different. The day after I submitted this manuscript to my editor, the story came true—the NHL was returning to Winnipeg! The true story didn't play out exactly as it does in *Faceoff* (which *is* fiction), but the basis of the story is accurate and the hockey fantasy is the backdrop for the romance fantasy between Tag and Kyla.

CHAPTER 1

Friday night. Six o'clock. A briefcase full of documents to review for the coming week that would occupy pretty much her entire weekend. Super fun.

Kyla MacIntosh rode the elevator down from the twenty-ninth floor of the Richardson Building, immune to the ear-popping speed of the elevator after years of working at the law offices of Ingram Howell Grant. Alone in the elevator, she leaned her head against the wall, then straightened and rolled her head, trying to ease the tightness in her neck that was causing a feeling of pressure around her head. The headaches were so constant now she barely noticed them, but at that moment she longed for some ibuprofen. And a massage. Her massage therapist was getting rich off her lately.

She came to a halt in the building lobby at seeing the pouring rain outside. Damn. With slower steps, she wandered into the hotel adjoining the office building to peer out the front doors. She set down her briefcase and purse and was about to slide her arms into the beige trench coat she carried over one arm when a burst of laughter from the lounge off the hotel lobby had her turning her head in recognition. Several of the lawyers from the firm sat on stools at a high round table, drinks in hand, laughing at something

1

one of them had just said. Including her mentor, senior partner Jim English, and her biggest competition for partner, Alex Covell.

She blinked at them. Damn. They'd gone for drinks without her again. She looked down at the gleaming stone floor, then back up. She pressed her lips together, lifted her purse and briefcase, straightened her shoulders and strode into the bar.

"Hey guys," she said, pasting on a smile. "I didn't know you were going for drinks tonight."

They all looked up at her, Jim, Alex and a few other partners and associates. "Hey, Kyla." After a short pause, Jim said, "Why don't you join us?"

"Thanks!" One of the men pulled another stool up to the table and she smiled at him as she climbed up onto it. "It's been a long week, I could use a drink."

The jocular conversation had come to a screeching halt and Kyla sighed inwardly. What had they been talking about? Probably her. She ordered a martini from the waitress with determined cheerfulness. "Pouring rain out there," she said. "Maybe by the time I've had a drink, it'll stop."

Reduced to talking about the weather. You could always talk about the weather in a city with four distinct seasons, where the temperatures ranged sixty degrees Celsius or more over the course of year.

"It's supposed to clear up for the weekend," Jim said.

"Heading out to the lake?" Alex asked him.

"Yeah. Pam's been up there all week. Jason and Lacy are bringing the kids this weekend," he said, referring to his son and daughter-in-law.

"How about you, Kyla? What are you up to this weekend?"

"Oh not much." She smiled. "Work."

They all made understanding noises. The conversation stuttered again.

She wasn't the only woman at the firm. There was, in fact, one female partner, but Kyla suspected Morgan had actually once been a man. Seriously. Not that Kyla had any issues with transgendered folks, but since Morgan had never married and, as far as anyone knew, had no family, she hadn't had to struggle with issues of maternity leave or trying to raise a family while billing as many hours as possible.

And inviting one of the female associates for Friday happy hour drinks wasn't apparently something her mentor felt comfortable with.

Kyla took a burning gulp of her martini.

"How's your golf game?" Hugh asked Jim. "Been out much so far this year?"

Kyla resisted the urge to roll her eyes. Jim somehow managed to golf in every big tournament in the city, which seemed to be a couple of times a week in the summer. Yeah, sure, it was networking, but geez.

"Yeah, I've been out a few times." Jim also had a membership at the most expensive golf club in the city and occasionally invited some of the other lawyers at the firm to golf with him there. He'd never invited Kyla, even though she'd made a determined effort to learn how to golf, knowing how much networking was done on the links. She despised golf, but saw it as a necessary business skill. Luckily she'd had her brothers and their friends to teach her.

The men started talking about putters and drivers, effectively shutting her out of the conversation. As usual. But she smiled and nodded and asked the odd question when she could, determined she was going to be part of this boys club.

A decision about who was going to be named the next partner at Ingram Howell Grant was being made this month. She and Alex were both considered the front runners. She'd been working her ass off for eight years for this and her plan to make partner was seemingly on track, but last week Jim had invited Alex to join him at a big golf tournament, making up a foursome with one of their largest corporate clients, and that had resurrected all her self-doubts. She hated that after months, even years, of feeling confident and on track, all of a sudden she was hyper aware of every

3

decision, every exclusion—like the lack of invitation to join them for drinks tonight.

Hell. This wasn't the first time that had happened. She'd become aware a long time ago that Jim wasn't comfortable asking her out for drinks. He was old enough to be her father, but their relationship wasn't father-daughter or even father-son, like his relationship with Alex was, and having drinks or lunch alone with her, or golfing with her, were clearly things he wasn't at ease doing.

She stared glumly down into her martini, momentarily diverted from her cheery façade.

"How about those Jets," Jim said. Everyone laughed. "Never thought I'd get to say that line again," he continued with a grin. "A toast to the Jets."

They all lifted their glasses and a chorus of "To the Jets" filled the air. People at the tables around them regarded them with amusement and then the entire lounge was filled with people shouting "To the Jets!" and lifting their glasses in a spontaneous toast.

Kyla couldn't help but laugh. The city of Winnipeg had never recovered from losing their National Hockey League team back in 1996 and the recent news that a couple of wealthy businessmen in town had finally succeeded in purchasing a struggling NHL team and were bringing it back to Winnipeg had created a buzz of excitement throughout the city.

She'd grown up with two older brothers who'd played hockey, although neither of them were good enough to turn pro, and her parents' best friends, the Hellers, had four boys who she'd practically grown up with as if they were brothers too. Three of those four boys now played in the NHL and the fourth had just been drafted. In fact, Tag Heller played for the team that was moving back to Winnipeg, which had added to the excitement. Return of the home town hockey hero.

She too had been following the story of the team's purchase in the news for months, interested largely in the complex legal and business issues that had arisen. She'd done a lot of legal work for the AHL team that had played in the city since the Jets had left and found the business side of professional sports fascinating.

The guys started talking hockey, but this was a subject Kyla was capable of participating in equally. She loved hockey. Then her BlackBerry bleeped in her purse. She pulled it out to glance at the screen. Her mother. She hesitated.

Guilt made her answer the call with a smile of apology at the men before she slipped off her stool and took a couple of steps away from the table.

"Hi, Mom."

"Kyla. Are you still coming for dinner tonight?"

Hell. She'd forgotten about that. "God, Mom, I'm sorry. I totally forgot. Why aren't you going out to the lake tonight?"

"We're going in the morning. We haven't seen you in…I don't even know how long it's been. You won't come to the lake, so at least come visit us tonight. We'll be at the cottage for the next few weeks."

"I've just been so busy. But, yeah, okay, I'll come tonight."

"We have some exciting news! So come as soon as you can."

"Okay. I'm just having a drink with some co-workers. Then I should go home and change."

"So…an hour?"

Her condo in the Exchange District was walking distance from the office and it would only take twenty minutes to drive from downtown to her parents' home in Tuxedo, but that still meant she had to cut this opportunity to socialize with the guys short. "Yeah. See you soon."

She returned to the table. "My mom," she said to the men. "I forgot I was supposed to go over there for dinner."

"How are your parents?" Jim asked.

"They're okay." Mom had recently undergone treatment for breast cancer, which had been a huge scare and stressful for everyone. "My mom's doing amazingly well. Dad's been busy as usual, traveling." Her father was the President and CEO of a large aerospace company.

She tipped her martini glass and drained the last of the drink. "I'd better head out." She smiled at the men as she again slid from her stool. "Have a good weekend, everyone."

"You too, Kyla."

In the lobby of the building, she surveyed the rain still pouring down outside. Damn. Walking to work was great when the weather was nice, even in the winter when it was cold, as long as you dressed for it, but three blocks in pouring rain was going to leave her wet even with her trench coat and umbrella.

She hurried along Rorie Street toward her condo in a renovated warehouse, head down, briefcase and purse bumping against her with every step, finally arriving at her building a bit out of breath. Man, she needed to get in shape. She'd never been athletic, but she knew the importance of staying fit and at one time had been a regular at the gym. But her gym membership had lapsed and working out had fallen to the bottom of her priority list lately, with work consuming all her time.

In her condo, she dropped her purse and case in the living room, hung up her wet coat and left her open umbrella on the rug in her foyer to dry. Luckily her car was parked underground, so she wouldn't have to go outside again until she got to her parents'.

In her bedroom she sighed as she changed out of her suit and into a pair of jeans, wishing she didn't have to go out. She was turning into a hermit lately and she knew it, but dammit, making partner was important. In a family of overachievers, she had to do this. So all she'd been doing lately was working, other than the time she'd spent at her mother's bedside following her surgery and then helping her at home as much as she could without missing too much time from work.

Even attending to a family illness wasn't looked favorably upon at the firm when they were in the middle of a big important case and she had partner in sight. She scraped her long hair into a ponytail, looping the elastic band around the hair to create a messy bun, surveying her face in the mirror of her dresser. She grimaced but didn't want to bother redoing her makeup just for dinner with her parents. They would love her no matter what she looked like.

Traffic was still heavy and slow-moving on Portage Avenue when she finally got there in her car, the wipers swishing back and forth across her windshield in a steady rhythm. The low clouds had darkened the sky and downtown streets were a smear of red and green and gold from traffic lights and tail lights, the colors bleeding into each other on the wet pavement. But as she left the downtown area, traffic eased and she made the trip to her parents' home quickly.

She parked on the tree-lined street, the dripping elms forming an almost perfect canopy of lush green above the road, then dashed up the sidewalk to the big old Tudor-style house. She didn't knock, just walked in. This was the house she'd grown up in, her home as much as her condo now was.

"I'm here!" she called, leaning against the door to close it. The alarm system beeped softly.

"Kyla!" Mom appeared at the end of the hall from the kitchen. "There you are!" They hugged and Mom drew back to study her. "You've lost more weight, haven't you?'

"Mom." Kyla pulled back and shook her head.

Worry darkened Mom's brown eyes. "You're so thin, honey."

Kyla smiled. "I'm fine, Mom. How are *you*?" Her mom's cancer diagnosis had given the whole family a huge scare.

"I'm great! Come in."

"Where's Dad?"

"In the family room. Come on. I just made pizza for dinner."

"You're not overdoing it, are you?"

"I'm fine," Mom said, leading the way. She'd faced an incredible challenge with strength and courage and an amazing attitude. She too was thin, having lost weight during her treatment, but she seemed to be back to her usual energy levels.

Kyla's dad rose from the chocolate leather couch in the great room where he was watching television while Mom bustled around

7

behind the big island that separated the kitchen from the family room. "Hey, sweet pea," he said giving her a hug. "How are you?"

She hugged her dad back and smiled up at him. "I'm good, Dad. Had to come for some of Mom's homemade pizza."

"Would you like a glass of wine?" Mom called.

"No, thanks. I had a martini after work and I have to drive home."

They chatted as Mom served up the pizza and Caesar salad.

"So what's this exciting news?" Kyla asked, sitting at the big island to eat.

"Oh! Scott's coming home! Next weekend!"

"Oh wow! With the baby?"

"Yes." Mom beamed. "And Jessica and Emily, of course. I'm so excited to see them."

Kyla's older brother Scott and his wife Jessica had just had their second child. Unfortunately the birth had happened right around the time of Mom's diagnosis and surgery and so they hadn't been able to travel home from Vancouver to see Mom and she hadn't been able to travel to Vancouver to see the new baby either.

"That's great! It will be nice to see them. I'll finally get to meet my new nephew."

"And there's more," Mom added. "I was talking to Doug and Laura."

Kyla nodded and lifted her piece of pizza to take a bite. Doug and Laura Heller were Mom and Dad's best friends. They lived across the street and also owned the cottage next door to her parents' up at the lake.

"They're pretty excited too because Tag's home."

Tag, the NHL player whose team was being moved back to Winnipeg. "I'm sure they are," Kyla said with a grin. "The whole town's excited."

"Yes! Of course Tag's moving back permanently, but the other boys are all coming home too. Just for a visit. Jason's coming from Chicago with his new girlfriend. Laura met her when they went to Chicago a few months ago. Matt's here for the whole summer and

Logan's home for a few weeks too. They put on that big charity golf tournament every year, you know."

"Yeah." She resisted the urge to roll her eyes. Another golf tournament. But this one she was definitely playing in, because it was the Heller brothers, after all. Her near-brothers. Though she hadn't seen much of them for quite a few years. It seemed like every time they were home, which wasn't that often these days, she was too busy with work to see them.

"So Laura and I had this great idea! We should have a big two-family reunion up at the lake! We'll all get together for a whole week and it'll be just like old times! Except of course Jessica and the kids will be there too, and now Jase's girlfriend."

Kyla's heart sank. It sounded like so much fun. But there was no way she could take a whole week off work just now. "That's a great idea, Mom." How was she going to break this to her, though? She sighed inwardly. "I wish I could come too."

As expected, Mom's face fell. She glanced at Dad. "You can't come?"

"You know I'm going crazy right now. They're making the decision about who's going to make partner in the next few weeks and I have this huge case I'm working on. In fact, I should be at home working right now."

Mom's eyebrows slanted down and her bottom lip pushed out a little. "Honey. You can't work all the time."

"I have to."

"Look at you. You've lost so much weight. You're pale, even though it's July."

Damn. She knew she should have taken a few minutes to fix her makeup. Maybe put on a little bronzer or something. Now Mom thought she was ill.

"You're a beautiful young woman. You should be out having fun. Dating. Coming up to the lake and relaxing on the beach."

Kyla's insides tightened up. The headache that had faded a little began to pound behind her eyes again, and her neck and

9

shoulders ached. "I'm sorry. Hopefully I'll get to see Scott and everyone while they're here."

"They're coming straight up to the lake from the airport," Mom said. "They're really looking forward to it. Emily will have so much fun there."

Did that mean she wouldn't get to see them at all if she didn't go up to the cottage too? She caught her lower lip between her teeth.

"Kyla," Dad said. "You look like you need a holiday. I'm sure taking a week off for a family reunion isn't going to jeopardize your chances of making partner. They've probably already decided and I'm sure you'll get it."

It could be true that they'd already decided, but she wasn't as confident as Dad was and didn't want to take the chance of screwing up this close to winning the prize. "It's just really bad timing." She pushed away her plate with the half eaten piece of pizza on it.

"Is that all you're eating?" Mom asked. "Kyla…"

"It's really good, Mom, as usual. I'm just not that hungry."

The worried expressions on their faces only made her feel worse. She felt guilty for disappointing her parents, but also felt sorry for herself that she was going to miss out on the fun of seeing her family and the Hellers. As a girl, she'd followed all six boys—her two brothers and the four Heller boys—around everywhere. Especially Tag. She had so many memories of those summers at the lake, not all of them good, but even the embarrassing ones had faded into less unpleasant memories with time.

"Tag will be living here now," she added. "I'm sure I'll see him some time."

"Your father is taking holidays," Mom said. "You know how hard it is to get him to take time off work."

"Guess that's where I get it from," she said with a bright smile.

Mom frowned. "I meant, if *he* can take time off for the family, then you should be able to." Her frown eased, replaced with a trembling bottom lip. Oh my god. Mom never cried. She'd been

10

through a cancer diagnosis and a mastectomy and Kyla had barely seen a tear. "You never know what could happen," she said. "This could be the last time we're ever all together as a family."

Oh no. Kyla stared at her, her insides going icy cold. "Mom, is there something you're not telling me? You're okay, aren't you?"

"Yes! I'm fine. I mean, as far as we know. I'm just saying, you never know."

She studied her mom's face. It was true. With cancer, you never knew. What if it came back? Oh my god. "I'll see," she said. "I'll talk to Jim on Monday and see about taking a week off."

Mom's face cleared and she blinked eyes that were just a little shiny. "Oh that's great!"

"Thank you, sweet pea," Dad said.

She nodded, still smiling. Now she really needed that ibuprofen.

CHAPTER 2

Tag Heller smiled and answered questions, acknowledging how happy everyone was about the team coming back to Winnipeg, acknowledging the team's abrupt ending to their season without even making the playoffs and the rebuilding they hoped to do in the coming year. He smiled but his temples throbbed and he really, really wanted a beer.

Since he'd arrived back in Winnipeg, it had been a nonstop whirl of promotional activity. Never mind finding a place to live or even unpacking in the bedroom at his parents' home. A thirty-one year old guy living with his parents. Nice. Really nice.

He'd looked at a few houses the realtor had shown him, but he had no idea what he was looking for and didn't want to make a rash decision out of desperation. He hadn't even sold his condo in Phoenix yet. The real estate market was still tough there after the recession. Luckily he had money and didn't have to rely on selling his old place, but still…it was a huge pain in the ass.

This press conference was wrapping up, thank god. One of the new team owners, Mike Glendower, was there, as was Brad Boscoe, the new coach. And this was only about the hundredth press conference he'd been at since arriving back in town a week ago. Okay maybe a slight exaggeration.

"Thrilled to be back in my home city," he said for the thousandth time. There was a lot of truth to it, but picking up and relocating was never easy, even when it was coming home. And there was a helluva difference between Phoenix and Winnipeg. Sure, it was summer now and the weather here was great, but in the dead of winter in forty below temps and the wind howling down Portage and Main, he'd be missing the desert sun something fierce.

He knew how much this meant to the city, more than any other player on the team since he'd grown up there and was fully aware of how devastating it had been to lose their NHL team. He'd been seventeen at the time, on the brink of embarking on his own pro hockey career. His home town Jets hadn't been the team he dreamed of playing for, but still, losing them had been a huge loss for the city. So this was monumental.

Even though the team had played crappy last year.

As the conference wrapped up, he rose from his chair and shook hands with some of the team personnel who were there. Everybody looked as happy as pigs in shit. None of the other players were there yet and Tag knew *they* weren't feeling so happy. Even as much of a pain in the ass it was for him, a single guy, to pick up and move, a lot of the guys had wives and families, kids in school with friends in Phoenix, and they were not so happy about moving. And especially to Winnipeg.

Which was why the team and the league were counting on him so much to put a positive spin on this for everyone—the league, the city, team personnel and the players. He'd always been a leader on the team, captain for the last five years, but now they'd told him he was the face of the new Jets.

Great. Just what he didn't want.

He just wanted to play hockey.

But it was July, and training camp was still a long way off. Meanwhile there was all the business part of hockey that had to be attended to, especially at this important juncture in the team's existence.

When he walked into his parents' home an hour later, his mom was in the kitchen making dinner. He headed straight to the fridge and helped himself to a beer.

"How did it go?" she asked him, rinsing some green beans in a colander in the sink.

"The usual." He drank deeply. "I'm tired of it already."

"I know." She smiled. "But you're doing great."

He grunted.

"I have some good news for you though," she said. "Scott MacIntosh is coming home next week with his new baby."

"Cool." He and Scott had been best friends pretty much their whole lives, although in the last ten years they'd only seen each other a handful of times. Scott now lived in Vancouver and their paths rarely crossed, although they kept in touch by email and on Facebook. Tag had only met Scott's wife at the wedding and one other time.

"I know! So Jenn MacIntosh and I were talking. Scott and his family are heading straight up to the lake when they get in. Jenn and Greg are going to be up there for the next three weeks on holidays. And we decided that we should all go up to the lake for a week. All our boys are home right now. All their kids are home. We could have a big family party up there. Doesn't that sound great?"

It did sound great. A week of chillaxing at the beach sounded like heaven. But he wasn't sure if that was possible right now. "I don't know, Mom. The team has all kinds of shit planned for me."

She gave him a look. "The season is months away. You can tell them to just back off."

He laughed. "Sure. I'll do that."

"Seriously, Tag. One week without you there isn't going to hurt them that much."

True. "Our golf tournament is in three weeks. We have to be back by then for sure."

"Of course. I already talked to Matt and Logan. Jase and Remi fly in Monday and I know Jase wants to take Remi up to the lake to show it to her. But you don't have to come until next weekend."

Huh. Jase and Remi. His little brother had gotten serious about a woman, and it wasn't the model he'd been dating for a couple of years, it was some little school teacher. But, in a bizarre twist, the supermodel ex-girlfriend was pregnant with Jase's baby. Tag had no doubt that the model had gotten knocked up on purpose in an attempt to hang onto Jase and his fame and fortune, and this new girlfriend would probably be next. Although Mom and Dad seemed impressed by her from the time they'd met her in Chicago.

No, Tag didn't envy Jase and his messed up life. He much preferred his single, no strings attached life.

"Okay, I'll see what I can do. Maybe we can rearrange some stuff."

She smiled. "Thank you. Can you imagine? It's been years since both our families were all together."

"Yeah. It has." Seeing old friends like Scott was good. Scott's younger brother Michael was the same age as Jase and they'd probably be happy to see each other again. And then there was Scott's little sister, Kyla. Tag couldn't help but smile at remembering her, how she'd trailed after the six boys, trying so hard to be one of them and how hopeless it had been. Poor little Kyla. Totally outnumbered by the boys. Totally outdone by them. All six boys had been athletic and energetic and she had been…not.

"Michael still lives here, right?"

"Yes that's right."

"Still single?"

"Yes."

"And how about Kyla?"

His mom looked at him with a smile. "You be nice to her."

He laid a hand on his chest. "When was I ever not nice to her?"

"You boys used to torture her unmercifully."

"She loved us."

Mom shook her head. "Maybe so, although I have no idea why. Anyway, yes, Kyla still lives here. She works at a big law firm."

"Oh, yeah. She did want to be a lawyer. She always was kind of geeky-smart."

His mom grinned and bent her head to the salmon she was sprinkling fresh dill over. "Geeky. Well. I guess you haven't seen her for a while."

He drank more beer, leaning against the counter. "Yeah. How long has it been? I don't even remember." Totally not true. He shrugged. "When's dinner?"

"About an hour."

"Okay. I'm going to take a shower. Matt and Logan and I are going out tonight."

"Ah." She nodded. "Behave yourselves."

"Mom. We're adults."

She gave a soft snort. "So's your brother Jase and that didn't stop him from getting into trouble."

Tag repressed his grin, remembering Jase's arrest a few months earlier. Really, getting arrested was serious stuff. It shouldn't be funny. Jase had caught hell from all directions for that little mishap. He couldn't wait to rib his little brother about it, though.

"Just remember," Mom continued. "The whole city is watching you now."

He sighed and clunked his empty bottle down on the granite counter. "Yeah. Thanks for the reminder."

Tag leaned against the bar at Harmony, loud music thumping in the darkness, strobe lights pulsing over the crowded dance floor. He lifted his beer to his lips.

"I'm too old for this," he muttered to his brothers.

"Yeah, you are," Matt said. "It's embarrassing, actually."

Tag's lips twitched. He shifted position and caught the eye of a girl at the end of the bar who was blatantly giving him the eye. She stood with two other girls dressed in skimpy halter tops and short skirts who were also looking at him and his brothers. She looked like she was barely out of high school. And she probably was. After living in the States where the legal drinking age was higher, coming to a bar here at home, where eighteen-year-olds were of legal drinking age, was a little disconcerting for Tag. The girl smiled seductively at him. Tag sighed.

Matt, at age twenty, fit in better with the crowd in the bar than Tag did. Even Logan, a few years younger than Tag, fit in better.

"I'm here to keep an eye on you youngsters," Tag said. "Mom was worried about you."

"About us? Bullshit."

Tag grinned. "Remember what Jase did a few months ago. Getting arrested isn't a good move. I think she's a little paranoid."

"No shit. What the hell got into him, anyway?"

"He was obviously hammered," Matt said.

"Obviously. But that's not like him," Logan said. "He's never been one to drink too much."

"He'd just found out that Brianne was pregnant," Tag said, remembering those phone conversations. Christ, Jase was going to be a father. Holy shit. Tag could barely wrap his mind around that concept. "We can give him a hard time about it when he gets here," he added, smiling at the prospect. "He flies in Monday."

"We can also bug him about losing the Cup to the Sharks."

"All the way to the finals and then couldn't do it." Matt shook his head.

One of the girls Tag had noticed earlier appeared beside him.

"Hi." She fluttered her mascara-laden eyelashes at Tag. "Can you guys settle something for me and my friends? I keep telling them that you guys are famous hockey players and they don't believe me."

Tag sighed inwardly and nodded. Matt smiled at the girl. "I'm not famous," he said. "But I am a hockey player."

"Oh." She looked confused, then looked at Tag. "But *you're* famous, right? You're Tag Heller."

17

"I am." He resisted the eye roll and smiled. "These are my brothers, Matt and Logan."

"I knew it! I saw you on TV the other day! You play for the Jets, don't you?"

"Yup."

Tag had no intention of flirting with girls, buying drinks or dancing. But apparently Matt did. The next thing Tag knew, the three girls had joined them, introducing themselves, batting their eyelashes and giggling. He couldn't bring himself to be rude to fans, even though these girls were probably more puck bunnies than true fans who'd be buying season tickets. He recognized the type after many years in the NHL.

He really was getting too old for this. Why had he agreed to come out to a bar tonight? He was tired and grouchy and that week at the lake away from all the attention and the need to always be "on" was sounding better and better.

CHAPTER 3

Kyla spent the rest of the week buried in work while fielding calls from various family members inquiring when she was coming up to the cottage, including her brother Scott, who'd called from Vancouver.

"Hey, dude." She'd broken into a smile on hearing his voice. "I hear you're coming home."

"Yeah. We'll be there Friday."

"Awesome! I can't wait to meet my new nephew!" She'd have to find time to pop out and buy presents for both the baby and her niece Emily. Except...she swallowed...what if she didn't get to see them to give them to them?

"I talked to Mom and she said you weren't sure if you were going to get up to the lake while we're there."

She sighed. "Yeah. I'm just looking at my schedule to see if I can rearrange things. Maybe you guys could all come into the city for a couple of days while you're here?"

"Maybe." He sounded doubtful. "I'm really looking forward to relaxing at the cottage. So, Kyla, you'd better be there."

"Oh, man. Now pressure from you too?"

"Mom says you're working too hard. She thinks you're about to collapse from exhaustion."

"I am not! Yeah, I'm working hard, but I have to."

"Look, Mom's been sick. I feel awful that I couldn't be there for her."

"I was here for her then." A faintly defensive tone crept into her voice.

"I know you were. But this is a chance for us to all get together. With all our schedules, and with Mom's cancer scaring the hell out of us all, this is really important, Kyla."

Her heart tightened in her chest. "I know it is. I'm working on it. Okay?"

"Okay. Good. Emily's all excited about seeing Auntie Kyla again."

"Sure, sure, play the guilt card," she muttered, rubbing her temples. "Mom already did that too. God, even Dad did! What is with you guys?"

"We love you," Scott said and she heard the amusement in his voice. "Not sure why sometimes, you workaholic bitch, but we do."

She laughed. "Thanks a lot. I'll have you know I come from an entire family of workaholics."

"I know you do. But lately…well, family's important."

"Becoming a father is making you go all soft."

"Yeah," he agreed. "That along with Mom's cancer. So we'll see you next weekend. Right?"

"I'll try."

It wasn't going to happen. She tried to figure out a way to rearrange things so she could take that week off and make her parents happy without pissing off her superiors at work. It hadn't looked promising, and then they'd announced they were going to name the new partner at the end of the week.

She hated to disappoint her family. And herself. But she was stuck in the city. In the office.

Then it was Friday, the end of the week, the day the decision was supposed to be made. She could barely concentrate on her work, so much nervous energy sizzled through her veins. She could hardly sit still. If she got partner, maybe she'd take the weekend off and go up to the lake just for a couple of days. So she could make the announcement and celebrate with her family. She smiled as she anticipated their reaction, her parents' pride, her brothers' teasing which she knew would hide their own pride in her. God, she *do* wanted that. She bounced a little in her chair. It would be the perfect way to announce it, even if maybe she did have to take some work with her to make it happen.

By mid-afternoon she was getting tired of waiting for it, so she wandered by Jim's office. The lights were out and the office was empty. She stopped at his assistant's desk. "Where's Jim?" she asked, frowning faintly.

"Golfing." Sandra smiled at her.

Kyla's eyebrows flew up. "Golfing? I thought they were announcing the new partner today."

Sandra tipped her head to one side. "Oh. Didn't he tell you? They decided to put it off for a few more weeks."

"What! No, he didn't tell me. He just told me on Monday they were going to do it this week."

Sandra shrugged. "I guess they changed their minds. Jim's on holidays for the next two weeks and the other partners start their holidays week after next. Nothing much will be happening around here until August."

Kyla fought down the pressure rising inside her, the disbelief and...yes, anger. "I see," she said quietly. "Thanks Sandra." Then she paused. "Who's he golfing with?"

"Alex, Hugh and Joe Pittman."

Kyla nodded, pressing her lips together. "Great! Nice day for it."

She returned to her office and stared out the window at the city twenty-nine stories below her, the prairie city spread out so flat you could almost see to the very edges of it, much of the urban landscape richly green with mature trees and parks.

Shit. Shit. Shit.

She'd spent the whole week there busting her butt trying to show them she was ready for the promotion, feeling sick with guilt about that, but determined to show everyone at the firm she was there...and they went golfing. Without her. And didn't even bother to tell her that everything had changed.

She tapped a pen on the desk. Her chest ached, the muscles in her neck and shoulders burned and even her jaw throbbed from clenching her teeth. Then she jerked when the pen in her hand cracked—she'd tapped it so hard on her desk she'd broken it. She stared at the broken utensil. More pressure built inside her. She wanted to get up and walk out. Just walk out.

She couldn't do that.

But she could do something.

She hit her computer keyboard and the monitor flickered to life. She pulled up her email program and started tapping away. Half an hour later, she'd rescheduled and delegated and sent out an email telling everyone she was going to be away from the office for the next week. She closed down her computer, started to put some files into her briefcase and stopped. She looked down at them. Her stomach hurt with that familiar gnawing pain. She needed this break. She wasn't even going to take work with her. She was going to the lake.

It was almost physically painful to leave the office empty-handed, but she forced herself to do it. Walking home along Rorie, she fought the anxiety that tightened her muscles to the point of making it difficult to breathe. This was going to be good. This would be fine.

In her condo, she didn't even bother to change out of her suit, just grabbed a suitcase and started throwing things in. What did she need for a week at the lake? A few bathing suits. A few pairs of shorts and tank tops. Flip flops. Sunscreen and a big can of bug spray.

She paused to download some books onto her digital reader, enough to keep her busy for a week of lying on the beach. No legal briefs or depositions or research materials for her. Just an assortment of romance novels by favorite authors she hadn't had time to read for a long time.

She hauled her suitcase down to her car in the parking garage, heaved it into the trunk of her little BMW and slammed the lid down. She was outta there.

Traffic was already getting heavy heading out of the city. Friday afternoon and everyone else was apparently getting an early start on the weekend too. Once out of the city and onto Highway 59, she pressed the gas pedal until the speedometer needle was at a hundred and five clicks, just barely over the speed limit. She had about an hour drive ahead of her and that was time to do a lot of thinking.

She could kick herself for being such a pushover, such a sucker that she'd sacrifice her personal life, her family life, for the firm, for making partner. But just because Jim and Alex were golfing together didn't mean anything. It didn't mean that Alex was going to be the new partner. But glumly, she couldn't help feeling it wasn't a very good sign. She turned things over and over in her head until the terrain on either side of the highway changed from scrubby to marshy as she neared Lake Winnipeg. Then she turned off the highway into the tiny resort town of Crystal Beach.

She was there. Even just driving down Main Street toward the public beach made her relax ever so slightly. She passed the familiar little businesses, the grocery store, the bar, the bakery, the tiny little movie theatre that only played movies on weekends. She let out a long breath. Disappointment still weighed on her, though, that she wasn't arriving here as a full-fledged partner in the law firm. She wasn't yet a big loser in that race, but she almost felt like it. Damn.

She turned onto Maple Street, then Bluebell Lane, a narrow tree-lined street that followed the curve of the lakeshore with cottages on either side. On the west side of the street the cottages backed onto the lake, and one of those cottages was her parents'. She had to smile at seeing all the cars parked in the small driveway and on the narrow road in front. Some of those vehicles likely belonged to the Hellers, who had the cottage next door. A little ripple of excitement ran through her at getting to see all those old friends and family.

She found a place to park. She hadn't called anyone to say she was coming. Maybe she should have. When she opened her car door, the freshness of the air filled her nostrils and she drew it deeply into her lungs—the combined scent of pine and freshly mowed grass and the faintly fishy smell of the big lake.

She approached the cottage, lugging her suitcase and taking in the familiar structure, a sprawling bungalow style painted white with neat grey shingles on the roof, black shutters on the windows and a bright yellow front door. She bypassed the front entrance, though, and followed the stone-paved path around the side, through a gate in a white picket fence covered with climbing pink roses, and around to the rear of the cottage, which she well knew was where everyone would be. There, the expansive wooden deck looked out over the grass sloping down toward the white sand beach, the lake spread in its magnificence just beyond that. The low sun drenched everything in vivid color, green grass, bright red, purple and yellow flowers hanging in baskets and overflowing out of pots, everything almost glowing. So beautiful.

The sounds of voices reached her as she rounded the corner of the cottage, people talking and laughing. Then she saw everyone on the deck, a whole group of very big, very gorgeous men all standing, some leaning against the railing, beers in hand. Dad played down on the grass with Emily, Mom reclined on one of the lounge chairs. Scott's wife Jessica sat in a chair nursing a baby and another woman Kyla didn't know occupied a chair next to her. Doug and Laura Heller stood near the house.

One of the men leaning on the railing looked up and spotted her.

"Hey! Kyla's here!" Her brother Scott grinned and everyone turned to look at her. She smiled at them all, so happy and relieved and excited to be there, to see everyone. And then that feeling of pressure rose up inside her again, so unexpectedly she couldn't get her breath. She tried to draw air into her lungs, but her head went light and dizzy. She put out a hand for the railing of the steps up to the deck, hoping it would help her balance, but her hand encountered only air and then her vision narrowed into a tiny circle of light before everything went black.

Tag stood on the deck of the MacIntoshes' cottage and watched the woman walking toward them, a suitcase bumping over the stone path behind her. Her long dark hair, parted in the middle, hung in curls and waves past her shoulders. A smile lit up her perfect oval face, her dark eyes smiling too. She looked a little out of place there at the lake in a black pencil skirt and a fitted white shirt that hugged her slender curves and—holy shit— amazing breasts, but she was stunningly gorgeous. *That* was Kyla?

Yeah. That was her. The smile was familiar, the way her eyes crinkled up when she smiled, the glossy brown hair. Then her smile faded, her face went visibly pale, almost green, her eyes went out of focus and then next thing they all knew, she was lying face down on the grass.

"Oh my god!" Jenn leaped out of her seat. Everyone else cried out, the guys cursing and hurtling down the steps.

"Auntie Kywa!" Emily came running across the grass. "Auntie Kywa! Is she dead?" She burst into tears.

The entire yard was a commotion of anxious cries and swearing and Emily's sobbing. Jenn called for her husband. "Greg, come quick!"

Tag reached Kyla first and gently rolled her onto her back. Her long hair spread around her head and her eyes fluttered. He touched his fingers to her cheek. "You okay?" he murmured.

Everyone else crowded around and Kyla's eyes opened. She stared up at them all blankly. "What..." she croaked. "What happened?"

"You fainted, honey," Jenn said. "Help her sit up, Tag. Push her head between her knees."

Tag helped her sit. He couldn't help but notice how her white shirt tightened across her breasts, how the buttons were undone low enough to see cleavage, and how her skirt had ridden up on her thighs, revealing spectacular legs.

"I'm okay," Kyla murmured, sounding dazed. With gentle pressure on the back of her silky head, he pushed her forward. "I can't really...do this...in this skirt."

No kidding. From where he knelt, Tag glimpsed red panties. He swallowed.

"Someone carry her up onto the deck," Jenn ordered. "Scott, you do it."

"Carry her!" Scott protested. "She'll break my back."

Tag snorted. Kyla looked like she weighed next to nothing, though she did have some nice curves on her. Scott was joking, of course. "Wuss," Tag said to Scott, lifting Kyla easily into his arms and carrying her up the five steps to the deck. He lowered her to the lounge chair where her mom had just been sitting.

"Oh my god," Kyla groaned. "I can't believe this." She put her hands to her still-pale cheeks.

"How do you feel, honey?" Jenn hovered beside her. "Hot? Dizzy?"

"Yes," Kyla whispered. She closed her eyes. "I was so dizzy. I couldn't breathe and I just got...light headed."

"You probably haven't eaten today, have you?" Jenn scolded, smoothing Kyla's hair back and laying a hand on her forehead.

"I did eat," Kyla protested feebly. "Um...I think."

"Oh lord," Jenn said. "I knew you were working too hard."

"I'm okay, Mom."

Tag shook his head and found the beer he'd left sitting on the wooden railing. She didn't look okay. She looked like she was ready to puke. What the hell?

"You're not okay," Jenn said crossly.

"Mom. Leave it alone right now. Okay?"

Tag didn't blame Kyla for not wanting to discuss her little health issues or whatever was going on with her in front of the whole crowd.

"Why are you here, honey?" Jenn asked. "I thought you couldn't come."

"I changed my mind." Kyla's eyes closed again, her head leaning back into the thick cushion of the chair. "I rearranged my schedule. I'm staying all week."

"Well, I'm happy about that," Jenn said. "But lord, you gave us a scare there." She looked around at everyone and gave a sheepish smile. "Sorry, folks."

"No need to apologize," Tag murmured, and everyone else assented.

"You remember everyone, of course," Jenn continued. "Tag and Logan and Jase and Matt."

"Yes." A smile whispered across her pretty lips. "Hi guys. Long time no see."

One corner of Tag's mouth tipped up. "Nice entrance, Mac," he said, calling her the nickname she'd insisted they use as kids. She'd tried so hard to be a tomboy. Never really pulled it off—it had been kind of funny. But cute.

She opened her eyes and focused on him. "Thanks." Their eyes met and held.

It had been a long time. Over ten years. Maybe twelve. Oh, they'd seen each other the odd brief time since then, Christmases when he'd been home. But the last summer they'd spent any time together he'd been...what? Nineteen? And her, eighteen? That would probably be about right. As a younger teenager, she'd followed him and his brother and her brothers around. He might've thought she had a crush on them—maybe even on him—except she'd grown up with them like a sister and had always wanted to be one of the boys.

But then one summer, things had changed. She'd no longer followed him, except with her eyes when she thought he wasn't looking. In fact, she'd tried to avoid him.

27

It had been sexual tension, pure and animal and hot, and he'd felt it for her too. But she was like a little sister to him, and holy crap, both her brothers would have beat the shit out of him if he'd laid a finger on her. So the sparks had flown, the heat had risen and they'd both avoided each other liked he avoided body checks from Dustin Byfuglien.

"I'm sorry," she said, dragging her gaze away from him to look at everyone else. "Didn't mean to cause such a commotion."

"Here's a glass of water, sweet pea." Greg handed her a glass.

"Oh, thank you." She took it from him and drank deeply, then leaned back. "Well. Where's my favorite niece?"

Emily squirmed down from her father's arms and ran over to Kyla. She laid a small hand on Kyla's cheek. "Are you okay, Auntie Kywa?"

Kyla smiled affectionately at the girl. "I'm fine, Em. Give me a big hug."

She wrapped her arms around the little girl, who squeezed her back, arms around her neck.

"I've missed you so much," Kyla said. "And I heard you got a new brother."

"I do, I do! Cay-web. He's right there, Mommy's feeding him. Bweastfeeding."

Kyla grinned at her sister-in-law, who had taken her seat again and still held the baby modestly beneath a blue blanket. "I guess I'll meet him in a few minutes once he's done eating. Hey, Jessica."

"He eats a wot," Emily said. "And he cwies and poops a wot too. And one day he peed on Mommy when she was changing his diaper."

"Boys." Kyla shook her head in mock disgust. "I bet *you* never peed on your mom."

Emily giggled. "No!"

Some of the worry and tension eased and Tag smiled at the interaction between Kyla and her niece. He'd never seen them together. He liked kids and he liked that Kyla liked them.

28

"You should get changed," Jenn said. "Do you want one of the boys to carry you in the house?"

"The 'boys'." Kyla smiled, sitting up straight. "No, I think I can walk, Mom."

But when she stood, she put out a hand to steady herself. Tag shook his head and moved toward her.

"No," she said. "I can walk." Her voice came out thready.

"Stubborn," he muttered. "Let me at least help you." He set a hand on the small of her back and guided her through sliding doors into the cottage. She crossed the spacious living area, a combination of living room, dining room and kitchen, toward a hall that led to the four bedrooms.

"I assume I'm in my usual room," she murmured.

Her mother spoke from behind Tag. "Yes, but Emily's staying in there," she said. "We didn't know you were coming. But Emily loves the top bunk, so you can have the bottom one."

"That's fine."

In the room she sank down onto the bed and lifted a shaky hand to her hair. She met Tag's eyes and grimaced. "Still feeling a little dizzy," she admitted.

"I'll go get your suitcase."

"Oh. Thank you."

Leaving the two women, he strode back outside and grabbed the case still sitting on the grass. The others out on the deck were all having a low conversation about what had just happened. "She works too damn hard," Michael muttered.

"Yes," Greg sighed.

Tag gave a grim nod and returned inside with the case. "Here you go," he said. "Where would you like it?"

"Oh. I don't know." She gestured vaguely. The bedroom wasn't large and Emily's things occupied a good deal of the space. "On the floor over there."

"I'll let you change, honey," Jenn said "Maybe you want to stay here and have a nap or something?"

29

"No. I didn't come to sleep," Kyla said with a frown. "I'm fine, Mom."

"Okay." Jenn backed out of the room with her forehead wrinkled.

Tag started toward the door too, then paused. He glanced out the door to make sure Jenn was gone, then turned back to Kyla. "What's going on, Mac?" he asked. "Are you pregnant?"

CHAPTER 4

Kyla gaped at Tag, there in her bedroom, a small bedroom that he seemed to fill with his large presence. Her heart picked up speed yet again and this time it wasn't the panic attack. It was him.

"No. I'm not pregnant!" she whispered, glancing at the door. God, what if Mom heard that? She'd *really* freak out.

As if she could be pregnant! She hadn't even been on a date in months. She rolled her eyes, but that made her head hurt and she groaned.

"What is it then?" he asked. "Your family seems to think you work too much."

"Okay. Yeah. I do. Everybody should just get over it. I'm fine."

His eyebrows rose. She sighed. She'd sounded like a real bitch.

"Sorry." She rubbed her forehead.

"What's wrong, Kyla? Are you sick?" His eyebrows now drew down above his strong nose. She immediately knew what he was thinking—her mom had just had cancer.

"No, I'm not sick." She softened her tone. She couldn't let him think something like that. "I...I've been having panic attacks."

She hated confessing that to him. Panic attacks were for fragile wimps who couldn't deal with life. The first two times she'd had

31

one, she'd thought she had heart problems and it had scared her enough to go to the doctor. When the doctor had told her it was a panic attack, she'd been insulted. But apparently that's what it was. She gave her head a disgusted shake. "I can't seem to help it. They come even at times when I don't feel stressed. I was all happy to come up here and see everyone and I get all the way here, and bam."

"Huh. Panic attack."

"Don't tell my parents!" She glared at him. "They don't need to know that."

His lips lifted into a small smile. "Okay. I won't tell them. Sounds like you need this holiday though."

"Yeah. Maybe. Hell, I don't know." She pushed her hair back. Had she done the right thing by taking off for a week? Maybe she'd overreacted to the delayed decision. Maybe this was a mistake. She should be there at the office Monday morning. She should have brought that work with her.

Her lungs started seizing up again and she forced herself to take slow, deep breaths.

Tag moved closer. "You okay?"

"Yes," she wheezed. "Damn."

"Maybe you should lie down."

He didn't have to convince her. Her head spun in woozy circles. She lowered herself to the pillow and stared up at the top bunk.

"This is so stupid," she muttered.

"You can't help it."

"I feel like I should be able to."

She jumped a little at the touch of hands on her ankles. Tag was slipping her flip flops off, the ones she'd exchanged her high-heeled pumps for at her condo even though they looked silly with business clothes. His fingers lingered on her feet for a few seconds and her skin tingled there.

"What can I get for you? More water? Maybe a stiff drink?"

She huffed out a laugh. "I almost feel like I'm drunk. I don't think a drink is a good idea. Oh, man." She closed her eyes. "You go on back out with the others. I'll just lay her for a while."

"You sure?"

"Yes."

"Okay." She heard his heavy footsteps walking out and tried to relax. Holy hell, she hadn't expected to react so strongly to seeing him again. She blew out a long slow breath. He was still so gorgeous. Still so freakin' big and muscular. Still had that wide sexy smile that tied her insides in knots and melted her panties.

She drifted a little, eyes closed. Memories floated through her head, memories of Tag, of those hot summers they'd spent at the lake. He'd been her favorite of the Heller boys, although she'd liked them all. They'd all been like brothers to her, teasing her and torturing her as brothers do, including her own, but then one summer Tag had suddenly seemed all grown up. They'd all been big, physically mature at an early age, but it seemed like overnight Tag went from being a bossy big brother to...holy crap, a hot guy.

It was funny how that had never happened with the others, maybe because they were younger than her. Logan was ten years younger, he'd always been the baby. Even though now he was six foot three just like the rest of them, maybe even taller. But Jase was only a year younger than her and although he and Tag looked so much alike, she'd never had burning lustful thoughts about Jase.

Just Tag. She gave a pleasant little sigh and rolled onto her side, burying her face in the pillow.

She awoke later, throbbing between her legs. Omigod, she'd been having a sex dream a really hot one. She slipped her hands between her legs. She'd been so close to coming, in her *sleep*. That hadn't happened for a while. She'd been dreaming about Tag, she knew it, even though the dream was rapidly receding into a nebulous haze, the details vague. She wanted to go back to sleep and finish it and have the orgasm she'd been so close to. Damn!

But she was awake now. It all flooded back, the embarrassment of fainting outside and having Tag carry her up onto the deck.

33

Heat slid over her body and she rolled to her back on the bed. God, she hated appearing weak. Collapsing like that just as she arrived was her worst freaking nightmare. Well, okay, it would've been worse if it had happened as she was walking into a business meeting.

Someone had closed the bedroom door at some point and she blinked into the darkness. She heard faint noises, conversation, laughter, music. The scent of steaks on the barbecue teased her senses and made her stomach rumble. She laid a hand there. When had she last eaten? She'd told her mom she had, but that Tim Horton's coffee and sour cream donut had been at...ten o'clock that morning. Gad, she was starving.

She sat up carefully, waiting for the wave of dizziness. But none came. She blinked into the dim room, then swung her legs over the side of the bed and eased her head out from beneath the top bunk.

She actually felt okay. Hungry, but okay.

She flicked the light on and found her suitcase, smiling at the Rapunzel doll, Cinderella's castle and Minnie Mouse beach towel on the floor. She pulled out a pair of knee length shorts and a T-shirt and quickly changed, grimacing at the wrinkles in her blouse. Ah, who cared. She crumpled it into a ball and shoved it into a corner of the case.

She checked the mirror before leaving, swiped her fingers over the smudges of mascara beneath her eyes, then dragged a brush through her hair. Okay. Presentable. Somewhat.

She followed the smell of food and voices back out onto the deck. The sun was just setting across the lake, sending shimmering rose and peach over the surface of the water and tinting the clouds. The trees down by the beach were dark silhouettes against the evening sky. She inhaled the fresh air as she stepped outside, cooler now, but still at least twenty-two degrees.

"Hey, sleepyhead," Michael called, spotting her. "You're up."

"Yeah. I guess I fell asleep."

She greeted everyone, this time properly, with hugs for Scott and Jessica and Logan and Matt and Jase. And Tag. As they moved closer, every nerve ending in her body went on sizzling alert. After that sex dream, she was hyperaware of him and his big, muscular body, his easy, sexy smile. She gave him a barely-touching hug and an embarrassed smile.

"You look better," he murmured. "Must've been reaction to seeing me again. I have that effect on women."

Her eyes flew open and met his, which held a teasing glint. "As if." She rolled her eyes. He grinned.

Jase introduced her to his girlfriend, a tiny little blonde named Remi. And Kyla got to hold her new nephew, Caleb, though he was sleeping. She gently rocked him in her arms as she smiled and talked to the others.

"Sorry about the drama," she said. "I don't know what happened. I guess I needed that little nap."

"Are you hungry, hon?" Mom asked. "I'll get you a plate. We just finished, but there's lots of food left."

"I'm starving." She smiled down at Caleb, admiring his delicate lips, blue-veined eyelids and long eyelashes. "He's gorgeous."

"Yeah," Scott said. "He looks like me."

Kyla snorted. "That is totally Jessica's nose. Thank god."

Scott grinned.

Kyla returned Caleb to his mother so she could take the plate of food from her mom, then sat down, setting the plate on her lap. She dug into a small steak, potatoes that had been cooked in foil with onions and garlic, grilled veggies and a salad dressed in tangy vinaigrette. "This is so good," she moaned. She looked up. "Is there any wine?"

"Is there any wine," Michael said. "Har. What would you like? Red? White? Chardonnay? Sauvignon blanc? Zinfandel?"

Kyla grinned. "Zinfandel sounds lovely."

A glass arrived and she set it on the wide arm of the wooden chair in which she sat. Little white lights twinkled in the tree near the deck as twilight descended. Crickets chirruped in the shrubs. A shout and a splash from one of the neighboring cottages reached their ears. Someone taking a late night dip in the lake.

"Tomorrow we're having a beach volleyball tournament," Logan said. "You in, Kyla?"

She caught the amusement in his eye. He was thinking about all the times she'd tried to play with them—volleyball, baseball, golf, you name it—and how hopeless she had been. "Sure." She tossed her hair back. She effing hated volleyball. No matter what she did, she could not coordinate things between her hands and arms and the damn ball. It never went where it was supposed to.

"Maybe you should take it easy tomorrow," Mom said, giving her an out.

She shrugged and cut another piece of steak. "Maybe."

She finished her meal, eating everything on her plate. She could've eaten more. Must be the fresh lake air giving her an appetite.

"Seconds?" Tag asked, leaning on the deck rail beside her, holding a beer loosely in his long fingers. "Or dessert?"

"There's dessert?"

He laughed. "My mom brought chocolate chip cookies and a couple of apple pies and ice cream. I think there's some left."

"Mmm. Sounds good." She started to rise and he held out a hand.

"Give me your plate. I'll go get you dessert. What do you want—pie or a cookie?"

She grinned up at him, handing him her plate. "Both."

"All right." He sound approving. He strode into the cottage with easy familiarity. They'd practically lived at each other's cottages, their parents taking turns hosting dinners and game nights, the boys having sleepovers. She watched his back, broad and muscular in a snug T-shirt, her gaze tracking down to his ass in a pair of beige cargo shorts. He had a great ass, firm and round. It was the hockey.

She shouldn't be admiring his ass.

He returned a moment later with another plate holding a piece of pie, a scoop of ice cream and three cookies.

"You don't need to wait on me," she said, pointlessly. He ignored her and handed her the plate. Once she'd taken it from him, he snagged one of the cookies.

"Hey," she protested.

He smiled. "You're never going to eat all that."

"I'm going to try." She picked up the fork.

She listened to the talk going on around her, a couple of different conversations, content to just eat her sweets and relax in the comfy chair, surrounded by friends and family and warm night air. She loved these summer nights, when it stayed light until ten o'clock at night and stayed warm until after dark, all night in fact. Mom lit up some citronella candles to keep the mosquitoes at bay. Now that it was darker, they'd start attacking. The flickering light added to the warm ambience on the deck and stars started to twinkle in the cobalt sky. That was another beautiful thing about being at the lake—once it got really, really dark, and that wasn't until at least eleven o'clock at this time of year, the sky was literally "milky" with the zillions of stars that you couldn't see in the city. She remembered lying in the grass with the guys, looking up at the sky, watching for falling stars. One year there'd been a big meteor shower and they'd seen shooting star after shooting star, so many that she'd given up making wishes.

A soft warmth unfurled inside her and muscles she didn't even realize were still tense relaxed even more. And that feeling of letting go kind of scared her a little. She'd hung on to all the tension and stress for so long, she wasn't sure what she'd do without it. What if she turned into a soft wimp?

"So what changed your mind about coming up?" Tag asked.

She shifted in her chair to look at him. Way up at him. "Oh. Just stuff."

He arched an eyebrow and lifted his beer to his lips. "Okay."

"So how are you doing? Happy to be back in the 'Peg?"

He gave a crooked smile. "Yes and no."

37

"Mixed feelings? Business or personal?"

"Both. It's been a long time since I lived here. Winnipeg's a small city compared to some I've lived in."

"You see it as a step down?" She'd read the news articles about the players' misgivings about moving to Winnipeg.

"No! Christ, no! Believe me, I'm not one of the guys who are complaining. That's part of the deal. You could end up anywhere. I feel so lucky to be making my living playing the sport I love—wherever it is." He laid a hand on his chest in a gesture that tugged something inside her. "I feel fucking...er, sorry..."

She gave a quick shake of her head and a smile. As if crude language bothered her, after growing up with six brothers. Sort of.

"I feel privileged," he continued. "To play the game I love. And to come home and play it in my home town..." He paused and she saw the genuine emotion on his face. "I'm not going to complain."

Warmth spread through her. She'd been annoyed by the attitude of some of the players coming to Winnipeg, how spoiled and entitled they'd sounded in their complaints. She should have known Tag wouldn't be like that. "So what is it? You're not married. Is there a girlfriend in Phoenix you're leaving behind?" She wasn't sure why she asked the question, striving to keep her voice casual. A sister would ask that.

"Lots."

She pursed her lips and he grinned again.

"It's a great move for the team," she said. "Seriously. And the league. With the dollar the way it is, you're not losing out money-wise. The cost of living is low here. You're going to do way better in terms of ticket sales, revenue...I've seen the attendance numbers at your home games and frankly, they sucked."

He gave her a level, appraising look. "Oh yeah?"

She returned the look. "What? You think I don't know the business? I've been following this whole story for months. Especially all the legal complications. I've found it quite fascinating." The sale of the team to the new owners had been a long, protracted endeavor that had drawn a lot of media attention, particularly the legal troubles that had arisen in Phoenix over their attempts to keep the team there.

He nodded slowly. "I guess I shouldn't be surprised that you would."

She tipped her head to one side. "I'm not sure how to take that, Tag. D'you think I'm stupid about sports just because I can't play them?"

He gave a slow smile that had heat trickling down through her body. "I've never thought you were stupid, Kyla."

The heat intensified, spreading through her chest. "Thanks."

"Coming home has actually been pretty stressful," he confessed, turning the beer bottle in both hands and looking down at it. "I'm really looking forward to this week up here to decompress and have some down time."

"Yeah." She sighed. "Me too. I guess." Then she tipped her head. "How come so stressful?"

"Well. This move is relatively easy for me, compared to some of the guys who are uprooting their families. But they've put a lot onto my shoulders—I have to put a positive spin on it for the other guys. And the media. We never got that much attention in Phoenix. It's just more than I'm used to." He eyed her again. "What are you stressed about, Kyla? To the point of having panic attacks."

"Sssh." She cast an anxious glance around to see if anyone had overheard. But the other conversations going on drowned out their quiet one.

"Sorry."

She looked at him and shifted again in her chair, sliding her butt down so she could bring her feet up and lean her head back, making it easier to look up at his height. "Stuff going on at work. They're going to be naming the new partner in the next few weeks."

"And that could be you?"

"Yes." Her stomach clenched. "I'm hoping. I actually thought it was going to be today. Which is why I thought I couldn't get away this week. Turned out…" She grimaced. "They postponed the decision and didn't bother to tell me. I've been working really, really hard for this and…" Anxiety knotted her insides. "Hell, I don't want to talk about work."

"No man in your life who gets annoyed about the long hours?"

She shot him a narrow-eyed look. "No. I don't have patience for men who get annoyed about my long hours."

He nodded. "Okay then. Let's neither of us talk about work this week. Let's just have a relaxing week at the beach, playing around, having fun, just like old times. Sound good?"

She eyed him and her stomach relaxed, the knot replaced by a slow roll of lust. No. Tag didn't mean anything like *that*. Old times meant when they'd been kids, just hanging out, running wild, swimming, waterskiing, catching frogs and building sand castles. Stargazing and sitting around bonfires roasting marshmallows.

Which all sounded wonderful too, scary wonderful, like that was a world she could never have again. She'd been so caught up in work, those times seemed like a dream, familiar and yet so unfamiliar to her lately that it was kind of scary. And that sex dream still haunted the edges of her mind and made her ache down low inside and Tag was still so very sexy and appealing. She nibbled her bottom lip.

"Yeah," she finally remembered to reply. "That sounds good."

CHAPTER 5

Sitting with the girls on the sidelines had never been Kyla's favorite thing to do.

But there she was the next morning, with all the girls—Remi, Jessica, holding baby Caleb, and Emily— watching six men play beach volleyball.

And it wasn't so bad. Two of the guys were her brothers and she ignored them, but the four Heller boys were oh-my-god gorgeous in board shorts and no shirts. They earned their living with their bodies. Well, the three older ones did; Matt was still in college, but he'd just been drafted and he'd soon be playing in the NHL too. So those bodies had to be in the peak of physical condition, and oh yeah, were they ever. Muscles rippled beneath skin that gleamed with perspiration in the sun. She watched Tag fearlessly dive for the ball, landing in the sand and rolling. With a shout of triumph, Matt spiked the ball over the net and it hit the sand before Scott could get to it.

"Damn," Jessica said.

Which team was Kyla cheering for? Her two brothers and Jase played against Tag, Logan and Matt. She should probably cheer for her brothers, but she couldn't take her eyes off Tag, and couldn't help but feel happy every time they scored a point.

She'd had more sex dreams about him last night.

That annoyed her, because she was still all tingly and achy and hyperaware of him. What was going on? This was crazy. It was like the last twelve years had disappeared and she was a lustful teenager for him all over again.

"I need more iced tea," she said. "Anybody else?"

"Can I come wiff you?" Emily asked, jumping to her feet.

"You sure can, sweetie pie. You can help me carry the drinks back. I bet those guys are thirsty too."

She and Emily trudged hand in hand through powder-soft sand back toward the cottage. Crystal Beach on the south shore of Lake Winnipeg had the finest, whitest sand, fine enough to be annoying when it got in everything, but there was no denying the beauty of the wide sandy beach.

"Daddy says I'm gonna wearn to wawer ski this afternoon," Emily said.

Kyla glanced down at her, startled. "Water ski? You?"

"Yes."

She blinked. "I think your daddy drank too much beer last night. Maybe he'll pull you on the tube, though. That would be fun. We could ride together."

Mom sat on the deck reading a book. "We came for drinks," Kyla told her.

"You should fill up that big Thermos jug." Mom set aside her book. "And take some plastic cups."

"Good idea."

A short while later, Kyla carried the jug full of iced tea and Emily carefully held a stack of plastic cups as they returned to the beach where the game was just ending. Tag swiped a beach towel across his face.

"Good game," he said to the others.

"Who won?" Kyla asked, pouring drinks.

"We did, of course." Tag grinned. "Man, I'm sweaty. I'm gonna go in the water." He guzzled back an entire glass of tea, nestled his cup in the sand and then headed to the lake.

"Good idea." Logan followed him.

Kyla watched Tag wade in. The lake was shallow here and you could walk out a long ways before it got deep, so she watched him, taking in his wide shoulders, the defined muscles in his back and his strong arms.

"It's going up to thirty-one degrees today," Jessica said.

"What's that?" Remi asked. "I'm only used to Fahrenheit."

"Hmm." Kyla thought. "I'm not sure. It's hot."

Remi laughed.

"That'd be high eighties." Jessica stood with the baby. "I'm going back to the cottage to change this little dude. Come on, Emily."

"It's hot already," Remi said. "A swim sounds like a great idea."

"Apparently we're going water skiing later," Kyla said. "Do you ski?"

"No." Remi grimaced. "Jase said he'd teach me how, but I'm not so sure I want to try."

"I haven't skied for a few years," Kyla said. "But it's fun."

Silence fell between the two women as they watched the guys cavorting in the water, too far away to hear what they were saying, although a burst of laughter reached their ears. Kyla looked at the petite blonde. "So. How did you and Jase meet?"

Remi turned toward her with a smile. "We met in a bar one night. I asked him to talk to me to keep my friend Delise from trying to fix me up with some random guy. Then Jase's ex showed up and he wanted *me* to talk to *him* to keep her away." A shadow passed over Remi's eyes.

Kyla shifted in the sand. "I...uh...heard that Jase's ex-girl-friend is pregnant."

"Yeah." The corners of Remi's mouth turned down briefly, then she smiled and met Kyla's eyes. Kyla dropped her gaze to the sand. She wasn't good at girl talk. Girls wanted to talk about things like clothes and shoes and men. Kyla would rather talk *to* men than about them. "It happened before we met. Like, *just* before. It's weird. But it is what it is."

"I guess so." The whole scenario raised a bunch of questions, but it didn't seem like a fun topic of conversation.

"Anyway, that was how we met, but we also ended up working together. Jase volunteers with a reading program and this past year he was at my school, working with my class."

"You're a teacher?"

"Yes."

Kyla grinned. "No shit."

Remi's eyebrows lifted, but she smiled. "You grew up with Jase. I guess you know what he thinks of teachers."

"Yeah. He had a rough time in school. It's kinda funny actually." She glanced back out toward the guys. "I'm going to give him a hard time about that."

"Oh…" Remi stepped toward Kyla. "I don't…"

Kyla looked back at the other woman. "Oh, don't worry. That's what we do. He's like a brother. He knows I love him. I mean… I don't *love* him. I…he's like a brother. You know. We're *supposed* to give each other a hard time." She paused. For an articulate attorney who had a reputation for presenting compelling arguments in court, she sounded like an idiot. She sighed. "He gave me enough grief in our younger days, believe me, I owe him."

Remi still gazed back at her with a worried expression. Damn. Remi was trying to protect him. Jase, the big guy, the fighter, the guy who'd protect anyone on his team, and that included the family team. Kyla'd seen it. She sighed. "Sorry, Remi. I guess you have to understand our families."

Remi's mouth tightened and her eyes narrowed a little. "Yeah. I'm just an outsider." She lifted her chin. "But if you hurt Jase…" She paused as if she wasn't sure what kind of threat to use. Kyla felt her lips twitch. The little pipsqueak wasn't exactly scary. Kyla almost laughed, but inside she also felt a pang of…what was that? Envy? That Jase had someone looking out for him like that? Jase, the last person in the world who needed protecting.

Or…maybe…*everyone* needed someone to look out for them. It was kind of sweet. Which almost made Kyla roll her eyes. And also feel a little burn of jealousy deep inside.

Stupid.

She smiled at Remi. "Don't worry."

The guys were coming back, wading through the shallow water, hair dripping. Tag lifted both hands to his head to sleek his hair back and the pose showed off his perfect shape, wide shoulders and chest tapering down to narrow hips. His board shorts rode so low on his hips it verged on indecent and Kyla couldn't drag her eyes away from there. Then Tag hooked his thumbs in the wet shorts and tugged them a little higher. She blinked.

Jase grabbed Remi and wrapped her in a big wet hug that made her squeal. "Oh my god, you're cold! You're getting me all wet."

He laughed and picked her up and started walking back towards his parents' cottage. Kyla watched them go, then turned back to see Tag, Matt and Logan exchanging glances.

"There they go again," Logan said. "Besides Mom and Dad, they're the only ones with their own bedroom."

"Where'd Jess go?" Scott asked.

"She took Emily and Caleb back to the cottage. Caleb needed a diaper change."

"Better go see if she needs any help." Scott and Michael both headed for the cottage.

"I'm hungry," Logan said. "Let's go find some lunch." He and Matt started walking down the beach too. "Coming, Tag?"

"Yeah. In a minute." He held the towel in his hands and stood next to Kyla. "How're you feeling today?"

"Good."

They were alone on the beach. Around the rocky point that separated the public beach from the cottages, the public beach was probably filling up with people, beach blankets and umbrellas, but here nobody else was out yet.

45

"You coming skiing later?" He rubbed the towel slowly over his chest.

"Sure."

"Mom's planning a game night tonight at our place. You're all invited."

Kyla nodded. "Cool. Just like old times."

"Yeah."

She studied him, his tanned skin gleaming in the bright sun, remembering the game nights of the past, how competitive he and his brothers were. And how competitive she was and how they'd had cut-throat games of Monopoly and Rummikub and Trivial Pursuit. She watched a drop of water slide down the side of his neck, then lower, slowly trickling down his chest. She wanted to go up on her tiptoes and lick that drop of water.

Heat suffused her body, and not from the noon sun overhead. Flashes of her dreams returned, hot glimpses of Tag naked, underneath her, on top of her. She swallowed. She lifted her gaze to his face and the heat in his eyes had her breath stalling. Tension arced between them as they stood there eyeing each other. When he looked at her mouth, her eyes went heavy-lidded and her heart began to thud.

"Oh man." He swiped the towel across his forehead, breaking the eye contact. She blinked. "Kyla."

"What?"

"Don't look at me like that."

"Um…like what?" As if she needed to ask. She wanted to eat him up. But did it show that much?

He looked her in the eye again. "Your brothers would kill me."

Her breath came in choppy little pants. Her insides went hot and liquid. "What am I supposed to say to that?" she said, her voice breathy. "We're not teenagers anymore."

"No. We're not." They were both remembering the last time this had happened. A long time ago. Heat built hotter between them.

She was used to going after what she wanted. She had a plan

for her career and she worked to make things happen. If she wanted Tag, why couldn't she have him?

Last time he'd tried to make a joke of it. As if he didn't want her. This time, older, wiser, more experienced, she could tell he did. Was he really going to let their families stand in the way of what they both wanted?

"My brothers have no say in who I..." She stopped. They'd been tiptoeing around it and when it came to saying it outright, she found she couldn't.

He smiled, that sexy lift of his wide mouth that melted her. She couldn't breathe. Her body thrummed with sexual tension. "Think about it, Mac," he said, his voice low and raspy. "We may not be teenagers but we're here with our families. Every bed in both our cottages is occupied. You're sharing a room with a three year old. I'm sharing a room with Matt."

She couldn't get air into her lungs and her heart thudded wildly against her ribs. She opened her mouth to tell him that she was very good at solving problems when she heard a little voice calling, "Auntie Kywa!"

She turned to see Emily appear on the path through the poplar trees edging the beach. "Shit," she muttered under her breath, but she plastered on a smile and reached for her niece as she hurtled toward her. She lifted her and propped her on her hip. "What's up, doodle bug?"

"Gwamma said to tell you we're having lunch."

"Okey dokey. I'm hungry." She met Tag's smiling eyes. "I'll see you later."

"Yeah."

Holy hell, this was crazy. What had gotten her suddenly so hot and horny, dreaming about sex when she was asleep, thinking about it when she was awake and practically ready to jump Tag right there on the beach? She pondered this as she carried a chattering Emily back to the cottage. It must be all pent up inside her or something, another effect of working too much. She needed to do something about it. But geez, even if she wanted to take care of

47

things herself, privacy was a definite issue, as Tag had so accurately pointed out. Damn.

Tag walked back to his parents' cottage along the beach rather than follow Kyla and take the short cut through the fence between the two properties. Jesus. He swiped perspiration from his brow that had nothing to do with the sun.

When she'd looked at him like that, with hungry, hot eyes, blood had rushed to his groin and his heart had pounded in his ears. If Emily hadn't shown up just then, he and Kyla would be rolling around in the sand.

He kicked the sand. What the hell was going on? Yeah, years ago he and Kyla had had a little heat happening, but he hadn't let anything come of it, although it had been pretty close that one night. So why after all this time was the heat even…hotter?

She was sexy as hell, that was why. As a teenager she'd changed from skinny kid with braces who tagged along with them and got in their way to a real girl with breasts and the sweetest ass, soft lips, silky dark hair and sultry brown eyes…he closed his eyes briefly as he headed up the path to the cottage. Now she was even hotter, a woman with the sexiest smile he'd ever seen, intelligence gleaming in those dark eyes along with lust.

There was no way they could do anything. That would be just crazy. Her brothers would kill him. Wouldn't they?

Waterskiing would take his mind off that.

But when Kyla showed up on the dock in a tiny little black bikini, waterskiing did *not* distract him from thinking about sex. And Kyla. And sex with Kyla. Holy hell. His gaze tracked down her body, from the round curves revealed in the V of the little halter top, to a bikini bottom that was so small he couldn't help but

48

wonder about what was beneath it and the wax job she must have recently had, 'cause, whoa.

He swallowed, grateful for the sunglasses that shielded his eyes and the baggy board shorts he wore as he turned to the wheel of the boat.

She covered up with a life jacket when it was her turn to ski.

"You still remember how?" Scott asked her, throwing the tow rope out. She grabbed it.

"I hope so! It's been a while."

She struggled a little to get up on the skis, finding her balance, but once she got going, she was fine. Tag was driving so he could only glance at her over his shoulder, leaving the others to spot her if she went down. She skied sedately in a straight line behind the boat for a while, then released the rope and sank into the water. They turned around and went back to get her.

When it was his turn, he couldn't resist showing off a little, skiing on one slalom ski, back and forth across the wake of the boat, turning backwards, spinning. He grinned, enjoying the speed, the use of his muscles, the adrenaline rush of it.

Then Kyla rode with Emily on the big inner tube, Emily's screams of excitement audible over the motor of the boat, Jessica watching anxiously, Scott laughing.

After an afternoon out on the lake, they all retreated to their cottages to shower and change and eat and then reconvened in the Heller dining room around a big oak table to play Trivial Pursuit.

Since there were so many of them, they formed teams of two, with one team of three, and Remi and Kyla ended up on a team. Jase folded his arms across his chest and regarded them glumly. "A teacher and a lawyer on the same team," he said. "How is that fair? We don't have a hope."

Tag gave him an elbow in the ribs. "Give yourself a little credit. We're not stupid."

Tag watched Remi share a glance with Kyla, then look back at Jase. "No, you're not," Remi said and Tag had the feeling she'd told Jase that before. Jase had always had that idea ever since that witch of a middle school teacher had told him that. Yeah, he'd struggled in school with his ADHD, but it didn't mean he was stupid.

The game began and soon turned into a cutthroat competition between Remi and Kyla and Jase and Tag.

"Science," Tag said when Remi's piece landed on a green square. "What is the largest mammal that ever lived?"

Kyla grinned. "The blue whale."

"Damn."

Remi pumped a fist as she collected a little wedge and put it in her circle.

"Roll again."

Kyla rolled the dice and moved.

"Entertainment." Remi glanced at Kyla.

"What is Radar O'Reilly's favorite drink?"

The two women stared at each other. "I have no idea," Remi whispered.

The two older couples snorted, earning a look from Kyla. "You know, I suppose?" she said to her parents.

"Of course. Don't you know who Radar O'Reilly is?"

"I know who he is," Kyla said loftily. "I just don't know what his favorite drink is."

"Beer," guessed Remi.

"Wrong!" Jace held up the card. "Grape Nehi."

"Whatever that is," Kyla muttered and everyone laughed.

"Sports!" Tag called triumphantly, landing on an orange square.

"How do you always land on sports?" Kyla complained. "Okay. Who played for the New York Rangers, the Brooklyn Dodgers and the New York Knicks in a single season?"

Tag stared at her, turned to look at Jase and got a blank look in return. "Rangers? Dodgers? Knicks? That's impossible. There's no one who's played for all those teams."

Kyla tapped her finger on her bottom lip in a very distracting way. Tag momentarily forgot all about sports.

50

"Give up?"

"Guess," Jase said to him.

"I got nothing."

Kyla grinned. "Gladys Gooding. The organist."

Tag groaned and fell back in his chair. "Shit!"

Laughing silently, Kyla slipped the card back into the box. The game continued until Kyla and Remi got the question, "Who shot Lee Harvey Oswald?"

Remi smiled and looked at Kyla. "You know that?"

"Jack Ruby."

"Yes!"

The two girls high-fived. "We win! This is fun!" Kyla said, wiggling in her chair. "Let's play again."

"We need to go put the kids to bed." Jess stood with the baby. Scott immediately rose too. "Good night, everyone."

"They get some alone time," Jase said with a look at Remi. Her cheeks went pink.

"You've got your own bedroom, what are you complaining about?" Tag said. "Hey, that reminds me. Mom, do we still have that tent we used to put up in the backyard?"

"Yes. It's in the shed. Why?"

"I was thinking I'd like to sleep out there. Matt snores and it's bugging me."

"I don't snore!"

"Yeah, you do." Tag grinned. "I'll find it later. Okay, one more game. We have to kick butt here."

"I'm out," Doug said. "You kids are too competitive for me."

The two sets of parents picked up their drinks and moved to sit on the couches, leaving Jase and Tag, Kyla and Remi and Michael, Matt and Logan.

"Okay. What does the C stand for in the equation E=Mc squared?"

Kyla turned to Remi wide-eyed. "Jesus. No clue."

"The speed of light," Remi said.

"Oh for...yes that's right." Michael grumbled as he returned

51

the card to the box and Tag caught the look of pride on Jase's face. His chest warmed inside. Damn. Seeing his little brother so happy and in love almost made him...nah.

The guys got the next one right and the intensity rose with each question. Kyla was bouncing in her seat most distractingly again. "You love this, don't you," Tag said to her.

She tipped her head to one side. "Are you saying I'm competitive?"

"Yes."

"I won't deny it. And right backatcha, Mr. We-have-to-win-the-Stanley-Cup."

"Sure, sure, rub it in. Jase came closest of any of us this year to winning the cup."

"Yeah, yeah," Jase said.

"Can you imagine?" Kyla said, rolling the dice. "If Jase had won the Stanley Cup and got to bring it home, along with the Jets coming back and Matt getting a first round draft pick...oh my god, the city would be going *crazy*!"

"Yeah, it's probably good you lost," Tag told Jase helpfully.

"Thanks, man." Jase lifted a hand with the middle finger raised, not high enough for his parents to see, but everyone at the table snickered.

Soon it was down to the last question for Tag and Jase to win. Matt read the question. "How many strokes make up a quadruple bogey on a par five golf hole?"

Tag closed his eyes, briefly, then said, "Nine."

"I knew that!" Kyla cried. "Damn!"

"We each won one game," Tag said.

"Let's play again!" Kyla said. Everyone else groaned. She slouched back. "Okay. Fine. I need another glass of wine."

CHAPTER 6

When Kyla finally rolled out of bed at nearly noon the next morning, fire burned her inner thighs and her legs gave out and she fell back onto the bed. Oh my god. The skiing yesterday had damn near killed her. Oh man, she was so out of shape. How pathetic. She managed to get to her feet and hobble to the bathroom. Her arms and shoulders screamed with pain at every movement. Lifting her arms to brush her teeth and her hair caused more burning across her muscles and she grimaced at her reflection.

She found the cottage empty and quiet. She hadn't even heard Emily get up. The guys had planned to go golfing at a nearby course first thing in the morning. The girls were probably outside or over at the Hellers'.

She found coffee still hot in the coffeemaker and painfully made herself a piece of toast and peanut butter. Jeez. She needed some ibuprofen or something. Thank god she'd turned down the golf invitation, though she'd been tempted to tag along with the guys like she always had. Today she was going to go down to the beach, on hands and knees if necessary, flop down on the sand and lie there for the rest of the day.

She changed into her pink bathing suit, the black one still

53

damp from yesterday, scooped up a bottle of SPF 30, slid her digital reader into a Ziploc bag to protect it from sand, and grabbed a towel and a beach blanket. With painful steps she made her way across the yard, through the poplar trees and shrubs, and onto the beach.

She spread the blanket and sat, her thigh muscles crying out as she lowered herself. She picked up the sunscreen. She wouldn't be able to do her back. Oh well. She'd just tan her front first. So she slathered up her front with sun protection, lay down, closed her eyes and breathed in the warm air. Some distant laughter and splashing and the hum of a boat out on the lake reached her ears. The sun warmed her face and relaxing heat seeped through her body. She sighed. Why had she not wanted to come up here again? She loved living in the city, loved restaurants and movies and concerts and shopping, hated leaving all that...but it was so nice here.

She might have dozed off a little, but awoke when a shadow covered her face. She cracked open one eye to see Tag sitting beside her on the blanket. "Hey." She tried to sit up, but gave up at the protest of her muscles and fell back down with a whimper. "You're done golfing?"

"Yeah."

"Who won?"

"Depends who you ask. Honestly, it was me. But it was close and I personally think all those other guys cheated.'

She laughed.

"Getting some sun, I see." The husky tone of his voice prompted her to open her eyes again. He was wearing sunglasses, but she could feel his gaze on her, studying her from head to toe. Her nipples tingled and tightened in the thin cups of her suit and her stomach did a little flip.

"Yes. Actually, I could use some help putting sunscreen on my back."

"I'm your man."

She went to roll over, but stopped with a groan. "Oh god."

"What's wrong? Are you sick again?"

"I was never sick," she said crossly. "I just have a few sore muscles today."

"From that little bit of skiing? Mac, honey, you clearly need to work out."

"Thanks so much."

"I don't mean you *look* like you need to work out. You look…" He paused and cleared his throat. "You look fucking amazing. But don't you go to a gym or something?"

"I haven't for a while." She pushed herself slowly over onto her stomach, painful knives stabbing into her muscles. "Too busy."

"No wonder you're so stressed. Exercise is the best way to deal with that." A cold squirt of liquid landed on her back and she twitched. Then he started rubbing it in with slow, sensual strokes. "Seriously."

"I know, but I'm busy. Some day I'll have time for that."

Some day. It seemed like a lot of her life was going to start "some day"—the day she made partner. Tag's hands moved up and down her back, pressing into sore muscles.

"Oh my god," she moaned.

"Feel good?"

"Mmmm." He kneaded her sore shoulders, his thumbs pressing into the hollows beneath her shoulder blades, his palms sliding with firm pressure down the ridges of muscles along her spine. "You're good at that."

"I've had a few massages," he said, sounding amused. "I may have picked up a few things."

"Oh yeah."

He kept massaging until she felt like she'd melted into a puddle of that sunscreen on the blanket.

"Where else is sore?"

"My…uh…thighs."

"Oh yeah. Skiing's hard on your abductors."

"Whatever."

His hands moved lower and began rubbing the backs of her

legs, pushing her legs apart a little in a gesture that had her pussy aching and her entire body tingling. His touch was firm but gentle enough that he didn't hurt her sore muscles too much. Then his fingers slid up under the edge of her bikini bottom onto her ass. She jerked.

"It's okay," he murmured. "Just making you feel good."

Oh, was he ever. She drifted on a cloud of sensual bliss at his expert touch until his fingers slid between her legs again. Oh hell, she wanted more there, wanted him to touch her where she needed it, where she ached. A tiny moan escaped her and she swore she could feel his smile. Then he bent over her and kissed her shoulder, a soft, open mouthed kiss that had another slow wave of lust rolling through her. God.

"You're killing me," she groaned.

"Am I hurting you?"

"No."

"Ah. Maybe you need your front done now."

"I did the front already."

"Well, the UV factor is high today. You should do it again." And he gently flipped her over like she was a doll. She gazed up at him with heavy eyes. He squirted a line of lotion on her chest, tossed the bottle aside and started rubbing there.

"Jesus Christ!" She jolted. "Oh, my god, my pecs! That hurts."

"Sorry." He smiled and gentled his touch, but kept kneading the tender muscles. "You need to do some pushups."

"I can't do pushups."

His smile deepened, and his fingers slid lower, down between her breasts over the soft flesh there. Her breath stuck in her throat and heat swept over her from her toes to her hairline.

His fingers paused. "This is crazy," he muttered. "Holy shit, Kyla."

"What?"

"I should never have put my hands on your body. Now I…" With his fingertips he gently massaged her breasts, right to the edge of the little cups, then just inside them…so close. Her nipples

56

stood at attention, hard and aching, but he didn't touch them, just massaged so slowly and carefully. She groaned again, her entire body tingling and alert. So much for the relaxing part.

"What?" she whispered again.

"I want to touch you everywhere."

"Oh." She wanted that too. She *ached* for that too.

He moved to her stomach, rubbing gently, then slipped his fingers just inside the top of her bikini bottom. "Tag," she breathed. His fingertips brushed against the triangle of hair she kept there and she gasped.

"I wondered what you had under your little bottoms," he said, voice gruff.

"Oh, god, Tag." Warmth unfurled inside her and her heart thudded in her chest. And then his fingers slid lower, over the fabric of her swimsuit between her legs, rubbing over her sensitive mound. "Oh dear god."

"Are you wet, Kyla?" he murmured. "You sound like you're getting turned on."

She whimpered. He cupped her pussy, so gently, then rubbed, and then his fingers slipped beneath her bikini bottom. Oh sweet Jesus, what was he doing? But all she could think was more, more, *more*. His fingers slipped over her slick folds. Yes. She was wet. She squeezed her eyes shut, her cheeks flaming. "You shouldn't..." she tried to say. "Someone might..."

"I'm watching. No one's coming. Except maybe you..."

"Oh my god." Her thighs fell apart to allow him access and his big fingers played over plump flesh, sending pleasure tingling through her veins. "You can't..."

He bent over her, fingers still between her legs, brushing over her clit, and he kissed her mouth, his head blocking the sun. "Kyla." His mouth opened on hers, his tongue licked her bottom lip. Oh god, oh god, pleasure hummed and buzzed where his fingers touched her, and heat slid over her body from his kiss. She lifted her arms to reach for him and dug her fingers into his shoulders.

"Tag, oh god, Tag…" Everything tightened into a sharp point of pleasure that shattered then and she gave a little cry against his mouth as he gave her the orgasm.

She lay there panting in the sun, letting him brush his mouth over her cheek, her jaw. "Nice," he said. "You needed that."

She wanted to punch him. She wanted to kiss him. She wanted him to do that again. And again. She reached for his leg, found bare skin, hairy muscular thigh, slid her hand up it beneath his shorts.

He made a choked sound and drew back. She smiled up at him, slipping her hand higher, his skin so soft there, and then holy crap, she encountered his hot, hard shaft. She blinked. She looked down at him. Good god, he was huge. Guess it made sense, since he was big everywhere. "Good thing these shorts are long," she murmured.

"Kyla," he croaked.

She got past her surprise at finding his cock so quickly, and stroked it. "Maybe you need this too." She curled her fingers around the thick stalk and rubbed her thumb over the head.

He hissed. Then he groaned. Then he went very still. "Don't make a fast move," he said, voice constricted. "But Matt and Logan are coming."

She couldn't help it, she jerked her hand out from under his shorts. "Oh my god."

"It's okay. They didn't see anything." He looked at her, arousal tightening his face. "Goddamn. Listen, Kyla. I set up the tent in the backyard. Come there tonight."

She sank her teeth into her bottom lip and stared at him. "Really?"

"Yeah. We can be alone."

"Tag…?" Her voice ended in a question.

"Hey, I thought you were going swimming," Matt called.

"We'll talk later." He rolled away from her and sat up straight. "I am," he replied to his brothers. "Just talking to Kyla for a minute."

"You're going swimming," she said. "You just finished golfing. Do you ever sit still?"

He grinned and jumped to his feet. "Nope." He held out a hand. "Coming in?"

"I can't move. My muscles hurt too much."

He went to his knees beside her, scooped his arms beneath her and lifted her.

"Tag! Put me down!"

"Want to get dropped into the water or want to walk?"

"I'll walk!"

He lowered her until her feet touched the soft warm sand. "Okay."

She followed them into the water, wading through it up to her knees, the shallow water pleasantly cool on her heated skin. She kept walking, the water climbing higher and higher, and when it touched her stomach, she tightened her belly muscles and went on her toes. Tag turned to look at her, the water still at his thighs because of his height. He grinned. "Coming, Mac?"

She gave him a look, up through her eyelashes, as if to say, *I just did, remember?* His eyes darkened and her heart fluttered. Was she really going to go to his tent tonight? "It's cold."

"Yeah, and I need that," he muttered. He strode further out, then jumped to do a shallow, perfect dive. She sighed once more at the male perfection of his body, his athletic grace. And taking a deep breath, she too dove under. Cool water closed over her head, shocking her body, stealing her breath, and she emerged with a gasp. But it didn't take long to get used to the water and she rolled to her back and floated, staring up at the blue sky and the clouds gathering right along the horizon.

"There you go," he said. "Swimming's good exercise."

She kicked her feet and splashed him a little. "Why are you trying to get me to exercise?"

"It's good for you. It's good for your body and your mind. And your soul. Actually the best exercise for all that is sex."

She almost sucked in a mouthful of lake water. "Okay then!"

59

She rolled and dove beneath the surface again, kicking hard. When she came up for air, she heard him laughing. She couldn't resist turning to look at him, the water glistening in his hair, his eyes gleaming, his wide mouth parted in a sexy smile that tugged a curl of heat inside her.

Oh god. What was he trying to do to her? He'd practically seduced her there on the beach, touching her like that, so intimately, and her pussy clenched at the memory. Now he was flirting with her.

Maybe he was right. Maybe some hot sex in a tent was just what she needed.

With Tag, though? That might be a big mistake. She'd had a secret crush on him forever. Sure, part of her wanted to know what it would finally be like. But the practical, sensible part of her was *afraid* of what that would finally be like. Also there was the family to consider. What impact would something like that have on the rest of their families and their friendships if she and Tag…oh lord.

She stroked through the water in a leisurely crawl, rolled onto her back and floated again. She'd had relationships with guys, quite a few in fact. But a serious relationship was another one of those "some day" things. She didn't have time for that right now. But maybe… soon. Depending on what happened with that partnership decision.

Or maybe she'd be even busier if she made partner.

Or maybe she wouldn't even *make* partner.

Her feet dragged along the sandy bottom of the lake, the ripples of sand bumpy beneath her feet, and she stood, the water only just above her waist here. She'd drifted back closer to shore. Logan had gone to retrieve a football.

"Wanna play, Mac?" Tag called.

She had to smile as she shook her head, wading out of the water. She couldn't catch a football if her life depended on it, despite the many times they'd tried to teach her. She'd tried so hard. "That's okay. I'm going to go get warm in the sun."

She toweled off and sat on her blanket, letting the sun dry her hair and warm her skin, watching three gorgeous guys throw the football and catch it with flexing muscles, taking fearless flying leaps into the water to grab it with hoots of laughter.

Remi appeared then. "Hi." She paused beside the blanket.

"Heya," Kyla said with a smile. "My Trivial Pursuit partner in crime. Have a seat."

Remi smiled with what looked like relief. "Thanks." She lowered herself to the blanket. "That was fun last night."

"It was."

"Thanks for...uh...playing with me."

Kyla turned back to look at her. "Uh...sure."

"I just...feel a little overwhelmed, sometimes. Trying to fit in with this whole family."

"I'm not family."

Remi tipped her head to one side. "Well, practically. You're all so close."

Kyla remembered their brief conversation and Remi's comment about fitting in. She'd never even considered how Remi felt in her first visit with the families. She sighed. She was so wrapped up in her own problems, she hadn't spared a thought for someone else. She should have been nicer to her. She sent Remi a smile. "You do fit in."

Remi smiled too. "Thanks. But I don't have the same kind of history you all do. It's just hard not feel a little excluded sometimes."

"Jase loves you. That's obvious. It just takes time, right? To build that history. It'll come. And his family all really likes you too. I can tell."

"Thanks. I really like them all too. Laura's been awesome."

"God, I love Laura." Kyla grimaced. "When I was a kid, she was what I wanted to be—a tomboy who could play any sport the boys could. I was hopeless at sports though."

"So am I." They exchanged a look of understanding.

"Did you know she played hockey?"

Remi grinned. "Yeah. I heard that. She is pretty amazing, dealing with all those men."

"Yeah. That's the other thing I admire about her, how she controls all those men without barking like a drill sergeant. She's like a second mom to me."

"See. You are practically family. Except...what's with you and Tag?"

Kyla blinked. "Me and Tag? Nothing."

"Uh-huh. He wasn't looking at you like a sister last night. There were a few times I felt like the rest of us weren't even there, the way you two were looking at each other and talking to each other."

"Oh. Oh god." Kyla bent her head and studied the fine grains of sand.

"You two aren't...haven't..."

"No!" Her stomach tightened. "But..." She glanced at Remi. She wasn't used to talking about stuff like this with other women. "Oh wow. Um." She didn't even know how to say it.

"You like him?"

"Well, of course I do."

Remi laughed. "Okay...do you want to do him?"

"Yeah." Kyla breathed out a long sigh. "I always have. From the time I was about fifteen years old."

Remi's eyes widened. "Really?"

"Don't say anything. Please. Don't tell anyone. I tried so hard not to let on. One summer, when I was about eighteen, Tag figured it out. But nothing ever happened because he basically turned me down." She made a face. "It was kind of humiliating."

Remi gave Kyla a slow, pretty smile. She was really sweet, Kyla had to admit. And smart. "I won't say anything. But I think he's figured it out again."

Kyla blew out a soft breath, remembering the near-sex-on-the-beach they'd had earlier. "Yeah."

62

CHAPTER 7

That night the Heller boys and the MacIntosh siblings all went to The Pelican, the bar on the beach. They sat on the big wooden deck, listening to the live band that played every weekend, drinking beer and coolers and talking. Matt met up with a group of girls that he knew from high school who were dressed in short shorts and skimpy tank tops and who were flirting outrageously with him. And he was flirting back.

Tag smiled and shook his head, lifting his beer bottle to his lips.

"This is so gorgeous." Remi gazed out at the lake being tinted pink and peach and gold by the setting sun. "It's like Lake Michigan."

"Not nearly as big," Tag said. "Lake Michigan is the third largest lake in North America. Lake Winnipeg is the seventh."

"Did you read that on a Trivial Pursuit card last night?" Kyla asked with a smirk.

He grinned. "No. I happened to know that. That's why I'm so good at Trivial Pursuit."

"We tied at one game each," she reminded him, leaning back in the white plastic chair she sat in.

"They're both huge lakes," Remi said. "You can't see the other

63

side, so it's big. And the sand is much nicer here. It's incredible, so soft and white."

"Yeah."

Tag watched Kyla lift one knee to prop her bare foot on the edge of the chair. She was wearing shorts almost as short as those puck bunnies hitting on Matt and a little T-shirt that hugged her breasts, the words, "I'm a lawyer, not a magician" printed on the front. Cute.

A hand landed on his shoulder and he turned to see Matt standing behind him. "Hey, dude," Matt said in a low voice, crouching beside Tag's chair. "Can I use that tent tonight?"

Tag frowned. "No."

"Why not? You're not seriously going to sleep out there, are you?"

"Yeah. I am."

"Look." Matt glanced at the girls. "All three of those girls want to…you know."

Whoa. "Not in my tent."

"But if I'm in the tent, my snoring won't bug you. You can have the bedroom all to yourself."

That wasn't going to work for what Tag had planned for the tent. "No way. The tent is mine." He already had his things out there, everything he was going to need later…

"Oh man! Come on! Three girls! At the same time!"

Tag caught Kyla's eye and knew she'd overheard when her lips twitched. She leaned over, her breasts brushing his arm. "Come on, Tag, think of your little brother."

He scowled at her, then looked back at Matt. "No. That's final. Find somewhere else for your…your…"

"Ménage à quatre?" Kyla suggested.

"Er…yeah."

"Shit." Matt stomped away.

Kyla laughed softly, still leaning near enough to him that he could smell her hair, a spicy floral scent mingled with a faint hint of coconut that remained from her sunscreen. Remembering applying that sunscreen to her sweet little body had him instantly hard as a hockey stick. He shifted in his chair. They had to get out of there and back to the cottage. Er, tent.

"I should get back and feed Caleb before we put him down for the night," Jessica said. She looked at Scott.

"I guess that means I'm leaving too." But he grinned good-naturedly as he rose from his chair. "Mom texted me a few minutes ago to say Emily was down."

"Your cell phone is working?" Jase asked.

"Yeah. Sometimes. The service is kind of spotty up here."

Tag snuck a glance at Kyla. Did she know what he was thinking?

A few minutes later, he yawned. "Well, I think I'll call it a night. Keep an eye on Matt."

"He's gone," Logan said. "He left with those girls."

Tag frowned. He'd better not find them in his tent when he got there. "Well, I guess he knows what he's doing."

Logan laughed. "Um, yeah. Pretty sure he does."

Tag glanced at Kyla, lifting one eyebrow, tossing some bills on the table to cover the tab. "G'night."

He strolled back toward the cottage down Main Street, then Bluebell Lane, through the growing darkness. The trees formed a lacy black canopy against the cobalt blue sky above him, where clouds were beginning to gather. The still-warm air brushed over his skin as he walked, a breeze springing up off the lake, and he breathed in deeply the fresh air scented with pine and grass and lake water. Would Kyla know to give it a few minutes and then follow him? Would she come?

Was he crazy to be doing this?

He wanted her with a deep visceral need that was almost shocking. It had started the moment he'd watched her keel over onto the grass on Friday night.

Well, no. It had started years ago. He'd just never really admitted it, to himself, to anyone. She'd somehow wriggled her way into his heart as a girl when she'd been so determined to keep up with them, despite her complete lack of athletic ability and coordination. She'd been so stubborn, so determined, so willing to do things that were clearly outside her comfort zone to fit in with them. Something had opened in his heart and let her in way back then.

It had turned sexual after that, when she'd grown up a little and he'd noticed that damn, she was hot. The one time they'd come so close to kissing, and he'd so wanted to, but he'd made himself back off. She was like a sister. Except not really. And her big brother was his best friend. Then Tag had left Winnipeg, had had lots of other girls, had focused on his career and had never looked back. Until she'd showed up here.

He crawled into the tent and turned on the battery-powered lamp he'd set on the small table. The tent was a decent size, and, unlike when he'd used it as a kid, his mom had recently purchased an inflatable bed, a double bed that, with the help of an extension cord plugged in at the cottage, had quickly filled with air and was pretty damn comfortable. A couple of sleeping bags zipped together—one was never big enough for him—and there was easily room for Kyla.

He stretched out on the bed, hands stacked behind his head, and stared up at the fabric of the tent. And waited.

Crickets chirped outside in the quiet night. The trees rustled in the breeze that had come up and cast shifting shadows on the tent. Somewhere an owl gave a low hoot.

Tag hadn't thought much about work since he'd been at the lake, but that was the whole purpose of coming there—to get a break. It was the off season, and while he usually kept busy in the off season working out and training, doing some hockey camps for kids and organizing their golf tournament, this year had been a little different and was likely going to be different right up until training camp started in September. Maybe he should feel guilty about taking a break in the middle of the craziness, but hell, they'd survive without him for a week, and more importantly...Kyla.

If she showed up here at the tent, it was meant to be. If she didn't...he could handle rejection. Maybe. It didn't happen to him very often, but he was under no illusions that he was that desirable. He had women after him all the time, but it was only because of who he was, what he did, how much money he made. He'd learned that the hard way. Since high school he'd been aware of the girls who chased hockey players, the ones who hung out at the arena, who waited outside classrooms where they knew the hockey players had classes, who stalked them to the bars or coffee shops they hung out at. They liked being associated with jocks, athletes, guys who had a little fame, maybe thinking that fame would rub off on them by association. He'd been shallow enough—and horny enough—to take advantage of that. Later in life he'd encountered those same women, now looking for marriage to a rich athlete. It was easy to get caught up in that kind of adulation and for a while he had. Hence his disastrous relationship with Jovannah.

Maybe that was one reason Kyla had managed to get inside him like that. As nearly one of the family, she'd never had that simpering, star-struck attitude around him or any of his brothers, despite their success. She'd accepted his hockey talent with a distinct lack of being impressed, much like his parents, who never made a big deal of it. His parents had always told him and his brothers they'd been given a gift and they had to work hard to make the best of it, but it didn't make them better than anyone else, and he'd always felt that from Kyla too. She teased and joked and accepted their hockey success with a matter-of-factness that... pleased him. He'd never really thought about that before, but now with some disappointing relationships under his belt, a little cynicism, maybe a touch of bitterness, her unimpressed attitude toward him made him feel at ease. Horny as hell, but at ease.

A rustle in the grass outside had his head lifting. It had to be either Kyla...or Matt with his three chicks...or maybe a skunk or a raccoon. He'd take Matt over the skunk any day, but hopefully it was...

A shadow darkened the opening of the tent and he caught his

67

breath, then rolled off the bed and unzipped the door. He reached out a hand, snagged a slender arm and yanked her inside.

Kyla.

"Hey!" She scowled at him in the pale golden light of the lamp.

"Quick," he said. "Don't let in the mosquitoes."

She rubbed her arm. "Yeah, I know. I think I got ten bites on the way here."

"They never bite me."

"I remember that," she said. "It used to piss me off. I'd pile on the DEET and still get attacked."

"It's because you're so soft and sweet." He moved closer. "My hide's tough, so they leave me alone."

"Uh-huh." She looked back at him uncertainly. "So…"

He grinned and with his body nudged her backward to the bed. It wasn't high, so her calves hit it and he caught her before she fell, lowering her to the mattress and then coming down beside her. "Tag…"

"Sssh. It's okay. No rush, Kyla. Let's just…make out."

She smiled. "You sound like we're in high school."

"Maybe we should've done this when we *were* in high school."

"You didn't want to. Remember?"

He paused. "Yeah." He'd been trying to do the right thing back then. "But that was a long time ago." Their eyes met and heat shimmered around them. His gaze dropped to her mouth. Her lips parted and he closed the distance between them and kissed her.

She made a soft sound in her throat and her lips clung to his. He lifted his mouth, tilted his head and kissed her again, deeper this time, opening his mouth on hers to push her lips open too, licking inside to taste her. He groaned.

They stretched out on the bed, her on her back, him beside her, leaning over her but not even really touching her. Other than the hand he cupped her cheek with.

"I'm still not sure about this…"

Assertive, confident Kyla was so sweetly uncertain, and that tugged at something deep inside him yet again. He rose up and looked down at her face, rubbing her bottom lip with his thumb. "I know, sweetheart."

Her eyes flickered at the endearment.

"We could just talk for a while," he said, despite his hard, aching cock. Her sweet kisses had made his blood run hot. "I'm not sure about this either. But we're not in high school. We're adults now. We both know what we want...right?"

"Yes." Her dark eyes gazed back at him, gleaming in the faint light.

"So what's wrong with it?"

"You know as well as I do. Our families."

"They don't have to know about this."

She sighed. "They'll know. Somehow. But even if they don't—what if this makes things all awkward between us? That will affect them."

He stroked her soft lip, rubbed his fingertips over her velvety cheek. "I don't want things to be awkward between us."

"I don't either."

He regarded her solemnly. "Do we stop, then?" His dick protested and every muscles in his body tightened.

She held his gaze.

"I don't want to hurt you," he growled. "But we need to be honest. I want you. Hell, Kyla, I can't explain it, except you make me so fucking hot for you." Her eyelashes fluttered. "But I'm not into relationships. Relationships haven't worked out so well for me in the past. And I've got a lot on my plate right now with this move."

She gave a tiny nod. "I know. I'm not looking for a relationship either. I'm trying to make partner and I don't have time for anything else in my life."

He wanted to point out to her how unhealthy that was, that there should be other things in her life—family, friends, time for herself, for fun, for her health. But since he'd also just said he wasn't into relationships, he pushed that thought away and said,

69

"Then we're on the same page. I know you feel it——we both want it. We want each other."

"Yes."

"Okay then…" And he kissed her again. Covered her mouth with his and took it, in a long, slow, heated kiss. Christ, her mouth was soft. And warm. And sweet. He licked along her bottom lip and then inside her mouth, slowly. Heat rushed through his body, an intense urgency that he had to fight to control. Slow…easy… they had all night.

All night. The thought made his body burn, his gut ache with longing for her.

He slid his hand into her hair, all silky, and bit softly at her lips. She let out a soft sigh of pleasure and then, finally, her hands came up to touch him too. One hand curled around his biceps, the other clutched his shoulder. Her tongue slid against his, delicate and warm, and more heat built inside him, low down inside him. He groaned.

"Jesus, Kyla," he sighed against her mouth. "I just wanna eat you up." An almost overpowering sexual hunger for her rose up inside him.

"I know, I know." They kissed again, mouths clinging, tongues playing. The temperature in the tent rose by several degrees even as the wind picked up outside, blowing the trees into dancing shadows, rushing through the branches in soft whispers and moans.

He shifted his mouth from hers and dragged it across her jaw, breathing in that coconut scent that smelled like sex on the beach, remembering fingering her to an orgasm earlier that day. And then she closed her teeth on his jaw and bit him, gently, and heat spiked inside him, hot and fast. Her tongue dragged across his skin and his mind blew up then. He moved over her, pushing her body into the air mattress with his own, on his elbows above her, holding her head with both hands, and he kissed her again, this time hard, demanding, urgent.

"Okay," he gasped. "Forget talking."

Her hands slid over him, down his back and then up into his

hair, back down to his ass. Her hips lifted against him, just barely, a supplication, and he pushed back, pelvis to pelvis, his dick hard and throbbing against her softness.

He hoped to god she didn't want to stop now, because it would fucking kill him. He slipped his hand down and found her breast. It filled his hand with lush softness, so perfect and soft beneath her T-shirt and bra. His head spun, blood pounded in his veins. She felt so good, and again he breathed in her scent. He gently squeezed her, rubbed his palm over the nub of her nipple. He wanted to rip her clothes off and get her naked, skin to skin, but... they had all night.

He opened his mouth on the side of her neck and gently sucked, licked and sucked again. "Mmm." Sweetness. "You taste so good, Kyla."

She made a little noise, maybe a word, he didn't know, he just kept licking and kissing her, making his way down to her throat where he rested his lips over the pulse that fluttered there. Then her hands found their way beneath his golf shirt and stroked over his skin. Tingles spread from her touch in radiating waves of pleasure.

"Want to feel your skin," she breathed. "And all your beautiful muscles."

He huffed out an amused breath. "You have some pretty muscles too."

He lifted his head and they shared a smile that stopped his heart briefly.

"I don't have muscles," she demurred, sliding her hands down to the base of his spine.

"Sure you do. They're not big and bulky, but they're there and they're really, really nice." He pushed the neckline of her T-shirt aside and traced his tongue along her collar bone.

She sighed again. "You're a good kisser, Tag."

"Thank you." He smiled against her skin. "So are you."

"Make that a *great* kisser." Her body shifted, her hips lifting again, and then her hands slid even lower, beneath the waistband of his cargo shorts, right onto his ass. He damn near burst into flames.

"I'm really trying to go slow," he gasped. "But you're making it damn hard."

She chucked. "I know. I can feel how hard it is."

He chuckled too, something expanding in his chest. They were both so hot for each other and yet could still laugh. It was fun, so much fun, being with her. He kissed her again, giving in to the delicious pleasure of it. He rubbed himself against her, letting her feel his hard on even more, because hell yeah, he was hard, *aching* hard for her.

He wanted to feel skin too, so slipped his hand beneath her T-shirt and laid his palm on her stomach, just resting there for a moment. "So nice," he murmured into her mouth. She licked his bottom lip, causing another surge of blood through his veins.

Then she was pushing at him, rolling him over, and taken by surprise, he let her do it. On top of him, she smiled down at him. "I don't want to go slow."

CHAPTER 8

Kyla looked down at Tag, almost overwhelmed by being with him like this, by his kisses so damn arousing, stirring up all kinds of weird sensations inside her, lust for sure, but also some kind of softer emotions, a tenderness, a desperate need for him—and she *liked* him, dammit. She'd been hesitant about this at first, but it had only taken a few minutes of kissing and petting and she was dying for him. Now.

She started to lean down to kiss him again, but found the tent spinning above her and then she was flat on her back again. She stared up at Tag. "Hey!"

"We're going slow."

A thrill ran through her, but she frowned. "Who died and put you in charge?"

He gave her a slow, seductive smile. "*I* put me in charge. Just because."

Her frown deepened. "That's not a good reason."

"We have all night," he murmured, kissing her jaw. "Slow is good."

She shoved at his chest. "But...but...*Tag*!"

He laughed softly and nipped her chin. "I'm bigger than you. How's that for a reason?"

"What are you? Some kind of Neanderthal dominant?"

"Hmm. Funny you should say that." He took her hands and lifted them above her head on the pillow, holding her there as he kissed the corner of her mouth. Heat washed down through her, a quivering excitement low in her belly at the way he held her down. She was annoyed though. Well, she *should* be annoyed. Oh hell, she was turned on. "I also have some ways of making you behave."

She gave a little snort, even as her insides melted at the touch of his mouth on the side of her neck. "Like what? Whips and chains?"

He smiled. Then he started kissing her again.

God, he was such a good kisser!

His mouth moved over hers with expert pressure and the perfect amount of tongue, his tongue sliding into her mouth so deliciously, so sexy and warm. His body big and heavy against hers heated her skin, pressed her into the mattress with sweet weight.

He slid his hands into her hair and kissed her again, and again. His mouth opened on hers, his tongue traced her bottom lip and she let herself fall into it, into the warm dreamy pleasure of it, the growing ache of desire inside her. She held onto his big shoulders, rubbing over them, his back, his arms. He felt so good.

His hand found its way beneath her T-shirt and when he touched the bare skin of her abdomen, her muscles there quivered. He stayed like that for long moments, just resting his hand there while they kissed.

The man knew how to torture a girl.

Her breasts swelled in anticipation of his touch, her nipples hard points. Finally his hand moved, rubbing in little circles while he slid his mouth over her jaw, nibbled her ear lobe and then dragged his tongue down the side of her neck. She shivered and her fingers dug into his back. His hand found her breast and cupped it again, but still through her bra. She wanted to sit up and rip her clothes off.

"I love how you smell," he whispered. "And your skin is so soft." She melted into the bed as he kissed her shoulder. Then he rose above her onto his knees, straddling her. He was so big and wide she just drank in the sight of him there as he pushed her top up, up, over her breasts. She helped him ease it off her arms and over her head, then let him reach behind her to unfasten her bra. He studied her as he tossed her clothes aside, then closed his hands around her waist gently, his big hands making her feel so small. "Wow, Kyla."

His words inflamed her, excitement twisting inside her, and her entire body pulsed with heat. She was so glad he liked looking at her. Her nipples tightened even more exposed to the air and his eyes and her lips parted as she looked up at him. His hands slid up her sides, then cupped her breasts, and when his thumbs brushed over her nipples, her body twitched hard. She moaned.

"So pretty," he muttered and bent his head. When his lips closed over one nipple, her eyes fell closed and her head tipped back into the pillow. Ribbons of pleasure streamed from nipple to womb and pressure built deep inside her.

She couldn't stop the noises that came from her throat and her hands dove into his hair, holding his head at her breast as he tugged at the sensitive flesh with his mouth. Everything inside her tightened, her hips lifted against his body as he bent over her. He moved to the other nipple and suckled there, slow and sweet.

She opened her eyes and lifted her head just as he looked up at her and their eyes met, his mouth on her breast, and the visual along with the sensations whipping over her nerve endings made her pussy spasm again with longing. "Tag," she whispered. "God, that's good. So good."

His eyelashes lowered and he sucked harder, just at the very tender tip of her nipple. She cried out at the exquisite pleasure of it while his hand found her other breast and rolled that nipple between his fingers. As he moved between breasts, sucking, licking, nibbling and pinching, she felt the folds of her pussy swell.

She knew from the deep ache that she was wet there, her clit pulsing with need.

Outside the tent, the wind picked up, tossing the tree branches with murmurs and whispers and groans that echoed the sounds inside the tent as Tag made love to her breasts until she writhed beneath him, desperate to have him inside her.

"So sweet," he murmured. "You have the prettiest breasts, Kyla. Perfect and round and soft. And your nipples…" He kissed one, then the other. "Love how hard they are. Just made to be sucked. Mmm." And he did that again.

The way he talked surprised her, this big jock, superstar athlete. She'd always known he was bright and articulate, the player the media all wanted to interview because he didn't talk in clichés and had thoughtful, intelligent opinions about his sport. But the low tone of his voice and the sexy words and compliments were unexpected. And so very, very hot. Burning, scorching, set-the-sleeping-bag-on-fire hot.

She let her hands roam everywhere she could, from his short silky hair to the soft skin at the nape of his neck, beneath the collar of his shirt to his big shoulder bones. Her fingers scrabbled in the soft cotton of his shirt to draw it up on his body so she could feel more skin, satiny smooth skin over hard muscle. Heat radiated from him, the same heat flowing through her body in waves.

He rose up then, reached for the hem of his shirt with crossed arms and pulled it up and off. She'd seen his bare chest, but now she got to touch it, sliding her palms up his ridged abs to his pecs, rubbing over the hair there and then his nipples, flat discs with hard little nubs. He groaned and came back down over her, this time to kiss her mouth again, but the feel of his chest against her bare breasts, skin to skin contact, sent flames licking over every nerve ending. She lifted her pelvis into him, his erection evident against her. He rubbed himself against her, so big and hard, and more flames built inside her, a deeper, needier ache that she was getting desperate to ease.

"Slow," he murmured against her lips at the restless movement of her hips beneath him. "Remember."

"I can't, Tag. God."

"Delayed gratification." He slid down her body. "Wait for it. It'll be worth it."

"Oh god. I hope so."

"Believe me, sweetheart." He kissed her throat. "It's killing me too." He laid a string of kisses down between her breasts and onto her tummy. Her muscles there tightened and her fingers curled into her palms on the bed beside her. He paused, his cheek on her stomach, another visual that would remain seared into her memory for always—Tag's tanned face, dark with a scruff of beard, his lips parted and eyes closed, resting against her naked body. So intimate. So heart-stoppingly beautiful. *Tag.*

A wave of emotion rushed over her. She tried to suppress it, squeezed her eyes closed against the prickling in the corners, and then as he moved again, pressing kisses to her abdomen, then lower, she got swept up in sensation again, in lovely warm sensation, Tag's mouth opening on her skin, his fingers unbuttoning and unzipping her shorts and parting them so he could kiss lower still, over the front of her panties.

She lifted her hips as he eased the shorts down over them and slid them down her legs. "Sweet," he murmured, looking at her panties, a pair of pink and white striped cheekie shorts. "Roll over."

She blinked at him and he made a circular motion with his finger. She huffed out a laugh and rolled onto her stomach.

"Oh Christ," he groaned.

"It's not like you haven't seen it before," she said, voice muffled by the sleeping bag. Her face heated, imagining his appraisal of her body. "In my bathing suit."

"True. But panties are different. Don't ask me why." A touch on her butt cheek made her jump a little and when she realized he kissed her there, heat rolled through her again. He kissed both cheeks, rubbed his palms over them and then, shockingly, slid his hand between her legs to cup her pussy. She moaned and her hips lifted and legs parted involuntarily to give him access, to touch her where she so badly needed to be touched. She felt him drawing her panties off, down over her legs.

She breathed into the sleeping bag, again imagining his eyes on her, what he was seeing.

"So pretty, Kyla." He stroked a finger through her folds. "Such a pretty pussy."

"I can't stand it anymore!" She tried to roll to her back again. "God, Tag!"

"Sssh. It's windy out, but someone could hear us."

She made a frustrated sound as his hand on her back pushed her down. God! With one hand he held her in place.

"I know what you need." To her surprise, he rolled off her and off the bed, leaving her bereft, her pussy aching and pulsing with need. Yeah, *she* knew what she needed and him leaving wasn't it. She lifted onto one elbow and watched him bend to pick up a small case from the floor of the tent. He set it on the bed, opened it and pulled out a roll of what looked like wide black tape.

"What is that?"

He smiled. He ripped open the roll. It sounded like Velcro. The next thing she knew, her wrists were bound behind her back with the stuff.

"Bondage tape." Satisfaction deepened his voice.

She blinked. Her wrists tingled.

"You can't be serious," she breathed into the sleeping bag. "What are you, some kind of sadistic perv?" She rolled over, bending her elbows and fitting her hands into the small of her back.

He tipped his head to one side and held her gaze steadily. "Maybe."

Her stomach did a little flip and warmth spread through her body. "I could just scream for help."

"Yeah...no. You won't."

"Why not?"

"Because you don't want anyone to know about this. And also because I have this." He pulled out a black rubber strap with a red ball attached to it.

Kyla stared. "What the hell is that?"

"A ball gag."

"Jesus." Her insides tightened and her pulse leaped. "You wouldn't do that."

"Not if you keep quiet." He held up the gag with a questioning look and a teasing glint in his eye that both excited and reassured her. The idea of trying to get away came into her head and then disappeared. Really, she had no hope of escaping him. And really...she didn't want to.

She opened her mouth, then closed it. "I don't want that," she muttered. "I don't want this stuff on my wrists either." She eyed the case. "What other kinky stuff have you got in there?"

He smiled. "This." He pulled out a small cloth bag. From it he withdrew a glass dildo. Her lips parted as she studied it. It was really very beautiful, clear glass with swirling red hearts in the shaft of it. She longed to touch it, to feel the weight of it, the smoothness of the glass. She swallowed. "Some lube." He tossed a small bottle onto the bed. "A paddle. A blindfold. Some other stuff...but I don't want to scare you."

"You don't scare me." Oh lord, anticipation curled deep inside her. Her eyes fell on the paddle.

His grin had her melting into her panties. "I know, dammit. I never have, have I?"

She cocked her head, unsure what that was about. "No. But why would you want to?"

"I don't want to scare you." He sat on the bed beside her and laid his hand on her chest between her breasts. Her nipples immediately tightened and her skin heated. "Sometimes I wish you were just a little more impressed with me."

She gazed up at him, not sure what to say. Didn't he *know* how impressed she was with him? How much she'd worshipped him?

"But then," he continued, his hand sliding up until it rested at

79

her throat, cupping her there, so gently, yet so compellingly. "I'm actually glad you're not. You treat me just like anyone else."

She continued to gaze at him, studying his face, trying to read what was behind these enigmatic comments. His hand on her throat made her feel...as if she belonged to him. Her heart beat faster. And harder. "I guess..." Okay, the brother comparison was just wrong now after what they'd just done. And truthfully, since she'd been old enough to know what sexual feelings felt like, that whole brother thing had been out the window. "I guess you're not that special," she finished.

His eyes widened, then narrowed—and then he laughed. "See? You fucking turn me upside down, Mac."

His use of that old nickname only stirred up her mixed feelings even more. She'd wanted so much to be one of the boys, she'd begged them to call her that. All the other boys had laughed at her, but Tag had started calling her that, and somehow, it had rubbed off on the others. She'd been forever grateful to him for that, for not making fun of her over it.

"Untie my hands," she said.

"No."

"Please."

"No."

"Tag..."

"Kyla."

She gazed back at him in frustration.

"Do you trust me?" He stroked her hair back from her face. "Do you trust that I won't hurt you?"

The answer sprang immediately to her lips, but she didn't say it. A question that important, that significant, deserved some thought. So she thought about it. And the answer was the same. "Yes."

"Thank you."

"But I like to be in control."

"Yeah. I know." One corner of his mouth kicked up. "But maybe it could be good to let go of control for a change. Hmmm?"

80

Resistance flared up inside her. She liked to be in control. She *had* to be in control. Being vulnerable and helpless like this made her feel…scared.

But yet, it wasn't Tag she was afraid of. So what was it?

She pressed her lips together, still studying his face. She'd known him most of her life. She knew his character—his reputation on the ice was the same as off the ice. He was known as an ethical player, someone who took responsibility, who stood up for others who needed it, who played by the rules, always did his best. He'd always been like that, on and off the ice. She knew she was safe with him.

"It'll be good," he said, still stroking her hair.

"I like to be on top."

He turned his head slightly and his eyes darkened. "We'll take turns."

A smile tugged at her lips and she gave in to it. "You always were so fair. And bossy."

The smile they shared had something soft and warm unfurling inside her, something big and expansive that made her throat ache a little.

CHAPTER 9

He was torturing both of them by prolonging this. But for some reason, he didn't want to go from zero to sex in two point five seconds. He wanted to turn her on, bring her up, play with her a little and make it so, so good.

He leaned over and kissed her mouth. "Just relax," he murmured. "Let me do this." Now that she was naked, he wanted to be too, so he rose and got rid of his cargo shorts and underwear. His cock sprang up and he gave it a couple of long, slow strokes as he moved over her on the bed. She watched him, her eyes on his hand, lips parted hungrily. Oh man.

He knelt between her thighs. She winced a little as he parted them and he smiled. "Still sore, sweetheart?"

"Just a bit. I'm okay."

"Good." He bent and kissed one thigh, smooth and soft, then kissed his way up to her hip bone, across her tummy to the other hip and down to that thigh. He stretched out on the bed then and gently pushed her knees back to reveal her to him. He studied her. Fascination with the female body filled him, along with admiration and intense arousal. What mysteries and raptures were hidden away between women's legs, so secret, so delicious. Pink and plump, her soft, hairless folds glistened with her own arousal. He kissed her there, soft little closed-mouth kisses up one side, and down the other. He nuzzled the tiny patch of dark hair, breathed in the sweet female scent of her. His mouth watered to taste her. He swallowed and rubbed his face on her thigh, his whiskers rasping a little on her soft skin. "Nice, Kyla. So beautiful." With his thumbs he parted her flesh, revealing deeper pink, more creaminess, and now he drew his tongue through the slit. Her body jerked and her fingers curled into the sleeping bag. Soft cries of pleasure filled the tent.

"Sweet." He swallowed her taste, licked her again, slow, long, lush licks, then kissed her clit. She cried out again. He played with her clit with his tongue, loving how it swelled and strained against his mouth, how she pulled her knees back even more. He slipped his hands under her ass and held her to his mouth, feasting on her with his lips and tongue and, so carefully, his teeth. "So sweet, Kyla."

"Oh god, oh my god." Her head turned from side to side on the pillow. "Oh, Tag, that's so good."

"You taste good, baby." He swiped his tongue over the softest flesh, her scent filling his head. "Oh man, Kyla. I wanna fuck you so bad."

"Do it!"

He looked up at her, his gaze tracking over her flat stomach and soft breasts, her arms still pinned beneath her. "Uh-uh. That just earned you more torture."

She whimpered and her teeth sank into her bottom lip.

"I was going to make you come," he continued, sliding a finger inside her. Wow. So wet. "But now you'll have to wait." He teased her with the very tip of his tongue, licked lower, nipped at her butt cheeks. "You have the sweetest ass, Kyla. Have I ever told you that?"

She made a little noise that might have been a no.

He loved how her firm round cheeks filled his palms. He

83

continued to lick her, slow and long, easing around her clit, but never on it. Her soft whimpers teased him and urged him on.

His thumb gathered up some of her cream and rubbed it around her puckered rear entrance. Her body twitched hard and she made a strangled noise. He looked up again to gauge her reaction. "Like that, Kyla?"

"I don't...know."

He wasn't sure if she said "know" or "no" so he did it again experimentally. Her moan of pleasure told him the answer. His cock throbbed with the need to be inside her, the thought of taking her there tightening his balls excruciatingly. But that would be later.

He flicked his tongue over her clit again. She sucked in a breath. He played there again, and when her thighs tightened and he felt her pussy clench, he drew back.

"Taaaag!" Her soft wail of protest made him smile. "I was so close..."

"I know." He moved up over her now, knees on either side of her body, until his cock was right at her mouth. Her eyes watched it, blinking rapidly. "Suck me, Kyla." He held his dick right at her mouth and rubbed it over her bottom lip. Her lips parted, so obediently, so sweetly, heat flared inside him. He pushed in gently, and when her mouth closed around the head, a ragged groan tore from his lips. His eyes fell closed as white-hot sparks whipped through his veins. "Aw, Christ, Kyla!"

Her little tongue explored the head of his cock while her lips wrapped around and she sucked greedily. Oh hell. For a moment he'd wondered if he was pushing too hard, but he'd seen the look of rapturous hunger on her face, and oh yeah, she wanted this too. He opened his eyes, eager to see the visual, to see her pretty lips on his swollen dick. At that moment she looked up at him, lashes framing her eyes like starbursts and he felt like he'd just taken a hard check into the boards.

His balls grew even tighter at the root of his cock, her mouth consuming him, sensation building at the base of his spine. "Sweet

Jesus," he muttered, watching her suck him with a look of such intense pleasure on her face he almost erupted. But no. He'd made her wait and he wasn't going to end this already, this way. She was going to come around his cock buried deep inside her and then he'd come too. He pulled out of her hungry mouth and she looked up at him and pouted.

He liked that. Exhilaration streamed through him as he reached for a condom, something else he kept in his kinky bag of tricks. He sheathed up and then rolled her to her side and unwrapped the tape from her wrists.

"Oh," she breathed, stretching her arms out. He took hold of her wrists and eased her arms up, ran his hands over her small muscles to ease any discomfort.

"Okay?" he murmured.

"Yes. Now I can touch you."

"Gonna fuck you now, Kyla." He once again moved between her legs. "Can't wait any longer."

He watched her face, watched the sweet smile that made her eyes crinkle up in a way that was so goddamn familiar and appealing.

"Yes, please," she whispered.

Something clenched in his chest. "Now *that's* the right way to answer," he growled, remembering her earlier command to "do it", and her smile deepened, so sexy and warm.

"I'm a fast learner." She reached for his shoulders. "And you're bossy."

"Yep." His voice came out gruff, but inside he was marsh-mallow soft and gooey at that fact that once again she'd amused him, right in the middle of hot sex. What a woman.

This was bad. This was so bad. He'd had a lot of good sex in his life, great sex even. Ménage sex, kinky sex, straight up vanilla sex. But he'd never had this feeling of falling, of sliding slowly into something deep and consuming, a feeling of overwhelming need to have this woman, to make her happy, to protect her from the world, from herself, from every damn thing. What the hell *was* that?

In a daze of lust and confusion he rubbed his gloved-up cock through her slick moisture, then pushed into her. Heat. He felt her heat through the latex, surrounding him, pulling him in deeper. He groaned, knees spread wide, hands on her thighs pushing them back. The soft noises coming from her throat inflamed him more, her hands reaching for him, pulling him to her.

"Oh god," she moaned. "Yes, yes, please Tag, fuck me. Like that."

He slid in further, her tight heat grasping his cock like a fist, and he fell over her, kissed her mouth with all the emotion swelling up inside him, sliding his tongue inside, again and again, as his cock slid in and out of her, wetness and heat, sparks and flames.

She felt so good, so fucking good, Christ. He pushed the hair back off her forehead as he kissed her and held her head and moved inside her, rocking against her. Her fingers dug into his shoulders, her nails a small bite of pain. "Kyla," he moaned. "Kyla."

She kissed him back, her mouth open for him, her tongue sliding against his. Did she taste herself on his mouth? The thought had more flames flickering inside him. Pressure built inside him, tingles at the base of his spine, his balls tightening. Oh man. Oh man. He was gonna come, soon, but she had to come first. Oh man.

He rose back up onto his knees, slid his hands to her waist and admired her as he thrust into her, slowing it down. Her breasts jiggled enticingly on her chest at each push and she lifted her hands to cup them. She pinched her own nipples, already so dark and hard. Fuck, that was hot! He tipped his head back briefly and fought for control.

Then he slipped a hand down to where they were joined, found her swollen little clit and rubbed. She made a soft noise, her hips moving against his, and once again their eyes met in a small explosion of heat and sparks, a magnetic connection that sucked him into a spinning haze. "There?"

She gave a jerky nod, and her eyes drifted closed. "Uh..." More sweet little noises followed, her pussy tightening around him, making him burn so hot. So hot. His veins pulsed with heat, flames licked over his balls and tingles raced up his spine. So close...he slowed his strokes while he rubbed her clit, breathing fast. He watched her face, so beautiful, flushed pink, her long brown hair spread wildly on the pillow around her head.

He felt her body tighten, her pussy clench around his dick and she gave a long, low cry of pleasure that had his heart nearly exploding out of his chest. "Oh yeah," he groaned, thrusting into her slick heat, feeling her pussy ripple around him.

She gave another soft wail and then she grabbed his wrist to hold his hand still. "Too much."

He got it, and moved back over her and kissed her mouth, slid his hands into her hair and fucked her with hard strokes. She met each stroke and sensation burned and twisted through his body.

"Damn, baby," he groaned against her lips. "Gonna come now too...oh Christ."

He let it come now, the orgasm that had been building, intense, barely controllable. His vision darkened, his body tightened and then pulsed inside her in, hot heavy spurts. A growl tore from deep inside him as he pressed into her, ecstasy erupting from inside him and flowing in heated waves of pleasure.

They stayed like that for a long time, her hands roaming his back, her lips pressing soft kisses to his shoulder and his neck. His lungs burned as he fought for breath, heart gradually slowing to a near-normal rhythm. Sweat dampened both their skins, and he finally lifted up to look down at her. He stroked damp hair off her forehead and their eyes met.

Whoa.

Her slow, sweet smile made something soft and hot expand inside him, so big he felt like bursting. He smiled back at her in response. "Wow." His fingertips moved over silky hair, soft skin.

"Yeah. Wow." Her hands ran over his ribs. "That was...wow. I came so hard."

Satisfaction swelled inside him now too. He kissed her lips. "Good." He moved inside her, his cock still hard, and her breath hitched in her throat.

"Still...sensitive," she whispered.

"Wanna make you come again." He nuzzled her hair and breathed in her scent, flowers and spice and coconut.

"Oh."

"In a few minutes." He gave one last thrust, then withdrew, reaching to hold the condom in place. "Let me get rid of this."

As he disposed of the condom in some tissues, Kyla let out a small shriek. "Eeep!" She scrambled into the sleeping bag and pulled it over her head. A moth had somehow found its way into the tent and fluttered around the lamp in dizzy circles.

Grinning, Tag captured the moth and quickly liberated it from the tent. "Afraid of a harmless little moth, Mac?" He climbed into the sleeping bag beside her. "It's gone."

She lifted her head. "I know they're harmless. I just don't like them flying around like that."

He smiled and pulled her against him. She curled up like a kitten, fitting perfectly to him, her face pressed to his throat. He drew in a long slow breath and let it out just as slowly. That had been kind of...brain-scrambling. Hotter than hot. He pressed his hand into the small of her back, bringing her closer still. His other hand slid into her hair and cupped her head.

He could stay like this forever.

"So nice," she murmured.

"Mmm."

For once he didn't want to go to sleep. Or go home, like he usually did after sex. In fact, he wanted to talk. He wanted to know all about Kyla, her life now, her job, everything. "How's your mom doing, Kyla?"

She stirred a little against him. "She's good. At least as far as we know."

"It must have been hard."

"Yeah." She talked, hesitantly at first, about her mom's cancer

88

diagnosis and the emotional roller coaster it had been for the entire family.

"It's good that you're all together this week."

She sighed. "Yes, it is. And I almost missed it."

"Because of your job."

"Yeah." And then she talked about that too, about the pressure she felt to succeed, the need to prove to her family she could do it too, her dad the CEO of a big successful company, her brother Scott already a VP of a major bank in Vancouver and even Michael, only twenty-eight, owned his own computer consulting business that was making him big bucks. She talked about the problems of fitting in at the law firm, the old boys club.

"You always wanted to be one of the boys." He let his hand wander down over the curve of her butt.

She laughed. "Yeah, that's true."

"But you're not one of the boys, Kyla."

She lifted her head. "What do you mean by that?"

"I mean…" He gave her a slow grin. "I wouldn't be here with you like this if you were a boy."

The corners of her mouth twitched upward. "No, I guess not."

"Seriously. You have some amazing qualities. Feminine qualities. You don't need to be one of the boys to be successful. You couldn't keep up with us when we played football or baseball or when we water-skied. But you had all of us wrapped around your little finger."

"I did not!"

"Sure you did. Remember that time you wanted to enter the sandcastle building competition? You had us all hauling buckets of sand and water and running around doing your bidding. And we loved it."

She went still against him.

"Maybe fitting in with the guys at work isn't the way to go. And Jesus, Kyla, if it's making you have panic attacks…"

She met his eyes again and her throat worked. "I'm fine."

"But is it what you really want?"

89

~

Kyla glared at him. "Why would you even ask that? Of course it's what I want! I wouldn't be doing it otherwise."

"Sometimes what we think we want isn't necessarily what's right for us, though."

She frowned at him. "What do you know about it?"

"I don't know anything about practicing law. But I know that you showed up here all pale and scrawny and immediately passed out on the lawn."

"Scrawny!"

He grinned. "Sorry. I take that back. You do look kinda thin, but you know I think you're gorgeous. But you've been having panic attacks and you don't have time for fun or exercise. That's not healthy for you. You don't even apparently have time for family since you weren't even going to come up here this week."

She didn't mention the headaches and stomach troubles she'd been experiencing for months. "It's what I've been working for my whole working life."

"No reason you can't change direction."

"I don't want to change direction. This is what I want."

"So you see yourself working at that law firm for the rest of your life? What's the name of it? Dewey Cheatham & Howe?"

She blinked, then burst out laughing. "Oh my god. It's Ingram Howell Grant. And yeah, I guess I do."

"What about a family? Getting married and having kids."

"I can do both."

"Of course you can, but will they support you in that? From what you've said, it didn't sound like they were all that supportive of you taking time off to be with your mom when she was sick. Will it be any different when you have kids?"

She couldn't answer that. There weren't a lot of female role models at Ingram Howell Grant. "I'll be a ground breaker. Once I'm partner, they'll have to respect me and what I need."

"Oh yeah?" He lifted an eyebrow. "You think that's going to

change just because you make partner? How do they make you feel now? Like a future partner? Or like you're a production machine? Do you feel valued? Or like you could be replaced?"

She didn't like those questions, and she had a sneaking suspicion it was because she wouldn't like the answers.

"Do they expect you to always choose the firm over your personal life?"

"They say they respect work life balance. And that sometimes personal things take priority. But..." She stopped, remembering the resentment she'd sensed when she'd taken time off to be with her mom, despite the words that had been said.

"Do you respect the senior partners at the firm?"

"Of course I do." Except when they went golfing and dumped work on her desk. "Oh just drop it, Tag," she said crossly. "I'm not all up in *your* business. I could ask you the same questions. You seemed pretty stressed last weekend. You didn't want to come up here either."

"I *wanted* to. I wasn't sure if I *could*. Yeah, I've been a little stressed with this whole move and the fact that we had a crappy season last year. I'm part of the team and I'm responsible for that and now coming back here, I know I have a big role to play in the PR aspects of it. But here's the difference...I love it. I love what I'm doing. I completely respect my new coach and the new team owners. Like you, I've worked my whole life for this, but I still love what I'm doing, every minute of it. And I'm not sure you do." He bent his head. "I'll admit there have been times in my life I've been scared about what I'd be able to do if I couldn't play hockey any more. It's good to be single-minded and focused on what you want, but that made me think—what if that's taken away from you? Because it can happen in a heartbeat. For me it could be a bad check—a head injury or my knee destroyed again." She remembered he'd been out for months a couple of years ago with a knee injury.

"Don't say that." For some reason her stomach cramped at the thought of Tag being hurt.

"It could happen. I have to face reality. For you, it could be going back to the city and discovering they named someone else partner. Then what would you do?"

She didn't know. She hadn't even wanted to consider what would happen if she didn't make partner. Would she stay on at the firm? Go somewhere else and start all over? What would be the odds of making partner somewhere else? "I don't know," she said quietly.

"I also have to face the reality that my hockey career is going to end a long time before your law career will. Then what will I do?"

She looked at him. "You're pretty practical, aren't you?"

"That makes me sound boring."

She moved her head side to side. "No, you're hardly boring, Tag." Not boring. Right now he was being annoyingly thought-provoking. He was making her think about things she'd been pushing to the back of her mind.

"Who's your competition?"

"What do you mean?"

"I know how competitive you are. Is there someone else competing for partnership?"

She lowered her chin and regarded him. "Yes. But that's not what it's about!"

"Isn't it? You've been competitive your whole life, Kyla. I've seen you do things you didn't really want to just to fit in with the guys, just to compete with us."

Her insides burned all the way up to her throat. She swallowed.

"I admire that about you," he continued softly. "You're determined and strong. You always have been. I have no doubt you'll succeed at this. I just think you need to take a step back and consider if it's really what you want." He smiled. "I've seen how happy your mom has been this week with her three kids and her grandchildren around. Family's important."

"You don't spend much time at home."

He eyed her curiously. "Forechecking, Kyla?"

She frowned at him.

"Forechecking—checking in the offensive zone with the intention of gaining control of the puck and setting up a scoring opportunity. Feeling a little defensive? Going on the offense?"

"This isn't a game."

"It's an analogy, sweetheart. Where's your sense of humor? I come home a lot, Kyla. Every summer. Other times during the year. I flew my parents down to Phoenix every year and a few months ago they came to Chicago to watch Jase and I play against each other."

Shame heated her cheeks. "I know. I'm sorry."

He leaned forward and kissed her mouth. "I'm sorry I called you scrawny."

"Okay, tell me about your crappy season."

And they talked about what a huge distraction the whole uproar over selling and moving the team had been for them pretty much all season, all the politics and media attention, then the actual sale and the move back to Winnipeg.

"D'you think all the talk distracted the players?" she asked. "Was that why you didn't have a great season?"

He gave her a long look. "Hell yeah. It was totally distracting, to everyone." He kissed her mouth. "You're pretty smart, Mac."

They talked for a long time, until Kyla's soft curves moving against him distracted him, heated his blood, hardened his dick, and then he rolled her over onto her back and kissed her in long, lazy wet kisses.

"Mmm." She bit gently at his bottom lip. "I thought you said I could have a turn to be on top."

He smiled down at her, that wide sexy mouth that made her insides flutter. "So I did. And that would be fair." He rolled off her and lay on his back. "Take me."

She laughed softly and laid a hand on his hard abdomen, shifting herself toward him. "Do I get to do whatever I want?"

"Um..." His dick twitched as she reached for it. "Maybe..."

"Maybe I need that bondage tape for you."

93

"Ha." She curled her fingers around his cock, so satisfyingly thick and hot in her hand. "I don't think that will be necessary."

"Hmm." She bent her head, teased him with her tongue, dragging it over the rim of his cock head, rubbing it against the underside, then licking down to the base and lower still, over his balls.

"Jesus Christ!" His hips jerked off the bed. "Oh, fuck, Kyla."

"Mmmhmm."

He reached for her hair, scooping it back and holding it loosely at her neck, she imagined, so he could see what she was doing. That pleased her. Pleasing him pleased her. She closed her eyes in delight and opened her mouth to take him in.

"Oh yeah, hell yeah, suck me," he groaned. "Suck my dick, Kyla, like that, so fucking good…"

She moved her mouth up and down on him, not taking him deep, there was no way she could; he was so thick in her mouth, so heavy on her tongue. She paused for a moment to absorb the sensation, the hot male taste of him. She grasped the base of his cock with one hand while the other played with his balls. Another rumble sounded in his throat.

"So nice." She lifted her head to gaze down at his throbbing shaft. "Very nice." Her thumb slid wetly over the head and Tag made a strangled noise. Then she moved over him holding herself above him.

"Condom," he croaked.

She paused. "Damn. Where are they?"

"In that case."

She slid off the mattress to the tent floor and rummaged around, returning with one held between two fingers. "I'll put it on."

"Sure."

She smiled at the thickness in his voice. A feeling of immense power rose inside her, feminine power, the power to please him with her touch. She paused for a moment, recalling his earlier words. This power felt good, so good. When she'd had her wrists bound, she'd felt erotically helpless but she'd also felt a strange

94

feeling of freedom——freedom and relief, to just be herself, to just feel, to not have to try to fit in.

She ripped open the package and rolled the condom on, torturing him by taking her time and then once again she rose above him. She closed her eyes as he entered her, stretching her with burning pressure, filling her with delicious heat. She laid her hands on Tag's muscled chest and moved on him, slowly easing his thick flesh inside her, little by little, until he was all the way in. She pressed a hand to her lower stomach, feeling voluptuously filled.

"Oh." She let out a soft breath. "Oh Tag."

"Oh yeah."

She rode him, eyes closed, then dragged her lids open to look down at him. He watched her with heated, hungry eyes that made her stomach swoop with excitement. This was so amazing, being with him like this. *He* was so amazing. He was dominant, controlling and he talked dirty and did dirty sexy things, but holy hell, she'd never been with a man who'd given her so much pleasure, who'd focused so much on her and her body. Her skin burned everywhere, her pussy flexing around his girth.

She lowered herself over him and kissed him, his mouth, his jaw, his neck, while his hands gripped her butt, moving her up and down on his shaft. Then one hand landed on her ass and heat flared. She gave a little cry, the sensation intensifying the tightening of her womb. Another heated caress on her butt drove her higher. Oh my god.

His fingers slipped between her cheeks, probing again at that back entrance. She cried out, his wicked touch there at that sensitive opening adding another layer of erotic sensation whipping through her body.

She pushed back up, touched herself, rubbed her clit, bit her bottom lip as sensation swelled inside her. She tightened her inner muscles even more on him, knowing that would do it, that would intensify her orgasm, and she fell onto his chest as it burst, pleasure sliding outward from that sharp point of ecstasy deep inside her. One of his hands came up around her shoulders, gripped her chin and turned her face to him and he kissed her, holding her like that as his hips lifted, fucking up into her fast and hard and so, so hot, and then he went taut and still beneath her, pressing his face against hers.

"Fuck, Kyla," he groaned against her cheek. "You fucking undo me."

She kissed his mouth again, hands on his face, kissed him over and over again in gratitude and longing and...what felt a lot like love.

CHAPTER 10

A distant low rumble outside the tent had Kyla lifting her head. "Was that thunder?"

"Dunno."

She snuggled into Tag's big warm body in the sleeping bag. He'd turned off the lamp and they lay there in darkness while outside the tent the wind howled in the trees in gusty bursts. Another, louder rumble told them the storm was moving closer. "It *is* thunder."

A flash of light briefly lit the tent.

"I love thunderstorms," she said, enjoying the feel of his arms around her, holding her against him.

"Ungh."

She smiled against his chest and rubbed her fingers over his big shoulder. They'd talked a lot earlier, but apparently he was all talked out and ready for post-coital sleep. She could probably sleep herself, feeling so relaxed and satisfied. "I should go back to the cottage."

"Don't go." His arms tightened. "It's starting to rain."

He was right. Big drops spattered on the tent, another flash of lightning illuminated them. Kyla counted in her head until thunder cracked. "Ooh, that's getting closer. That was loud." She liked storms, but she didn't want to be running across the yard through one. "Are we safe here, Tag?"

"Of course."

"There are trees all around us. What if one gets hit by lightning?"

"We'll be fine." He kissed her temple in a sweetly tender gesture that made her insides go all soft. "Want me to distract you again?"

"I don't think you're ready for that yet. You're not a teenager any more, you know." His hand landed sharply on her ass and heat flared there. "Hey!" She wriggled against him.

"Keep that up and I'll be ready, all right," he growled.

The storm passed over them with rapid flashes of light, crashes and cracks that made the ground shake. "Wicked," Kyla breathed, so glad she was wrapped up in Tag's arms. There was no way she was going to sleep with that raging on outside the tent, so she just let herself enjoy it, snuggled into the sleeping bag and Tag's body. He stroked a hand lazily up and down her back.

A complicated mixture of emotions filled her. Tenderness. Affection. Sexual satisfaction. Maybe when you put those all together it felt like love. But it couldn't be love. They'd both agreed at the start of this that neither of them was looking for a relationship. This was about sex, about finally fulfilling one of her deepest, longest-standing fantasies—being with Tag.

It was nothing more than that.

Her chest ached a little at that thought, but she ignored it and squeezed her eyes closed. The fast-moving storm was now only faint flickers of light and muted rumbling, although rain drizzled down steadily outside, and she closed her eyes and let herself drift off to sleep.

Day came early at this time of year, the tent growing bright shortly after five in the morning. Kyla blinked and turned her head to look at Tag, spooned around her, his hand resting on her stomach, her butt pressed into his groin. His eyes remained closed and she studied him, his long eyelashes, thick straight eyebrows, his square jaw deeply shadowed with whiskers. She gave a shaky smile at how beautiful he was and how moving it was to be there with him like that. How incredible last night had been.

The brightening light outside told her that the storm had long since gone and the sky was clear. She needed to get back to the cottage before people started getting up and realized she'd never come home. She started to flip back the edge of the sleeping bag, but Tag's hand tightened on her stomach.

"Where're you going?" he mumbled.

"Home. Before someone realizes I wasn't there all night."

He sighed and kissed her shoulder. "Damn."

She gave a little huff of laughter. "I know."

"I should get up and go for a run."

"Good god, Tag. It's five in the morning!"

"It's good to go before it gets too hot. Come with me."

"Are you kidding me? I'm going back to bed to sleep for a few more hours. Or six."

He smiled against her skin. "Running's good for you. You need more exercise."

"I'd never keep up with you."

"Okay, I'll go again later. When you're ready."

"You're insane."

"I have to stay in shape. The off season isn't for sitting around on my ass drinking beer."

Warmth unfurled inside her and she touched his stubbly cheek. "As if you'd ever do that."

"Seriously." He rubbed his face into her palm. "You were trash talking me last night about getting old, but the truth is…I am."

"You're not old!"

"I'm not young either." He gave a wry smile. "I have to work even harder than some of the young guys to be ready for training camp. And I swear every year it gets harder."

"Oh, Tag. You're in amazing shape."

One corner of his mouth kicked up. "Why thank you. I like your shape too."

They lay there smiling at each other, cocooned in a flannel-lined sleeping bag in the slowly brightening tent.

"I'll take you fishing this afternoon," he said.

She blinked. "Fishing?"

"Sure. In the boat."

"Um…okay. Maybe we could bring Emily."

"No."

She lifted one eyebrow and he gave her a sexy grin. "Don't get me wrong. Emily's a doll. But I want to take you fishing…alone."

Memories of other fishing trips with the guys flooded back, how she'd tried so hard not to be horrified by the poor fish wriggling with a hook in its mouth, how the poor fish had died, how the guys had taken gruesome pleasure in gutting and filleting the poor fish and then had expected her to eat it. She'd almost been in tears, but as usual, determined to be one of them, she'd made herself do it. She did not want to go fishing. But if it was with Tag…

"Okay." She kissed him quickly, then slipped out and found her clothes, cool and slightly damp from the morning air. Ugh. She dressed, aware of his hot gaze on her as she did so.

"Wear that black bikini," he said.

She paused, then hid her grin as she ducked out of the tent and jogged across the wet grass.

"So where are the fishing rods?"

Tag steered the boat into a small bay a few miles up the shore from Crystal Beach. A patch of reeds waved lazily in the afternoon breeze, the sun glinting off the water. Kyla moved to the back of the boat and stood there with one hand on the back of a seat, balancing in the rocking boat.

"I didn't bring any."

She looked at him over one bare shoulder. She'd worn the little halter-topped black bikini as he'd asked, but also wore a pair of loose black board shorts over it. They hung low on her hips, emphasizing the smooth curves of her waist.

"You didn't bring fishing rods? How are we going to fish?"

"We're not. I hate fishing."

She gaped at him. "You hate fishing?"

He grinned. "I'm happy to eat all the pickerel the others catch, but it's really not my favorite thing to do."

"Then why did we come here?"

He just looked at her.

"Oh." Her mouth curved. "Really? In the boat?"

He cut the motor and silence surrounded them, save for the soft slap of waves against the boat. "We're alone," he murmured, moving toward her. "That's all I care about."

She laid a hand on his bare chest and smiled up at him. "You are a bad, bad man."

"I know." He bent and kissed her. She wore some kind of fruity lip balm that tasted sweet and he licked her mouth. "I did however bring towels, blankets and extra sunscreen. We wouldn't want you to burn any areas that aren't...ahem...used to sun exposure."

Her cheeks turned a pretty pink.

"We should probably take care of that first." He reached for a bottle of sunscreen. "I kinda like putting sun lotion on you."

"I kind of like it too," she murmured.

"Take your top off."

She blinked at him, then surveyed the area around them. They were completely alone. She bit her lip. "This is kind of...public."

"There's no one else here. We'll hear a boat if someone comes."

She dragged her tongue across her bottom lip, then reached behind her for the fastener of the top. It loosened and she lifted it over her head. Tag's breath stuck in his throat for a moment as he surveyed her naked, there in the boat, the sun gleaming on her dark brown hair, her skin smooth and golden, her breasts so firm and perfect. Her nipples puckered into tight brown points.

Tag's dick had been half hard all day thinking about this, and it hardened even more in his shorts. He squirted lotion into his hand, then rubbed his hands together before setting them on her chest. She gave a little moan as he massaged the cream into her breasts, slowly, enjoying the slippery feel of soft flesh in his palms, the way her breath hitched as he rubbed over her nipples. There was something a little wicked about doing this out in the open in broad daylight.

"Pretty tits," he murmured. "Very pretty. Now take off those shorts. And the bottom."

Her cheeks even pinker, she unfastened the shorts and let them drop to the floor of the gently swaying boat. With her thumbs under the sides, she shimmied out of the bikini bottom and stood before him naked.

Ah holy hell. "Better do your back," he muttered, squeezing out more sunscreen. He balanced his ass against the back of one of the seats and widened his stance to rub lotion into her back, all the way down to her sweet little butt. "Cute tan lines. You tan easily, don't you?" She hadn't had much color in her skin when she'd arrived a few days ago, all office-worker pale.

"I guess." Her voice drifted in the afternoon sun, followed by a soft sigh of pleasure as he massaged her.

"Me too."

"Do I get to put sunscreen on your ass?"

He chuckled. "That's the plan, sweetheart."

"Yay."

He grinned, turned her to face him and finished off by rubbing cream onto her stomach and hips, as low as he could get, brushing over the little patch of dark curls. Fuck, this was turning him on unbelievably. "There you go. Should be good for a little while."

She continued to cast apprehensive glances out at the water and he liked that she was a little on edge. That just added to the excitement. Although he had a feeling it didn't matter where he and Kyla were, there'd be plenty of excitement.

He dropped his own shorts, exposing his throbbing cock to the sun and Kyla's gaze and oh yeah, her touch. She reached for him immediately with both hands, looking at him with such awe and appreciation she made him feel like a god. He groaned.

"Oh yeah, sunscreen," she whispered. He gave her his back and let her small hands rub him all over from shoulders and neck all the way down to the base of his spine where his skin prickled, and then lower. "Lean forward," she directed him and he set his hand on the back of the seat and bent at the waist.

Her hands were playful and naughty, rubbing over his ass cheeks, then between, then lower, making him suck in a sharp gasp. When she touched his balls from behind, heat rushed through his body. He tried to rise and turn around, but she laid a hand on his back to stop him.

"Wait," she said softly. "This is fun."

Fun, oh hell yeah, wicked sexy fun. She tortured him with her delicate touches on his testicles, firmer caresses on his buttocks and then reached between his legs for his raging hard on and gave a tug.

"Fuck!"

Her body pressed up against his from behind as she stroked him like that, the coconut scent of sunscreen invading his senses, the bright sun blinding him. He liked foreplay, but not this time. He pulled away from her, whirled around and grabbed hold of her naked body, all shiny from the lotion, hauled her up against him in a move that sent the boat rocking and kissed her hard. She wrapped her arms around his neck and kissed him back, mouths sliding, tongues licking, their gleaming bodies gliding against each other.

He turned her around and eased her down onto the seat of the boat on her knees. "This is so crazy." She gripped the back of the seat and glanced over her shoulder at him seductively.

"Crazy hot. Look at you, all shiny and naked." He moved up behind her and nudged her thighs farther apart, revealing her sweet pussy. "So gorgeous, Kyla." He drew his fingers up through her slit, testing. "And wet."

She moaned. He spread her legs wider, one hand pressing on

her back, and adjusted her position so he could find her entrance and slid inside, slowly, carefully. Christ, it only got better, hotter, every time. Her head fell back and exquisite pleasure streaked through him as she surrounded him in liquid heat. So fucking hot, scalding his dick. Then..."*Shit*." He went very still, his body pulsing.

"What?"

"I forgot condoms. Fuck! I can't believe that."

"You knew we weren't going to be fishing. How could you forget that?" Amusement tinged her voice.

"I'm sorry, Kyla." He leaned over her and touched his forehead to her shoulder, fighting for air.

"Do it anyway."

He went still.

"I'm on the pill. Lord knows why, I haven't had a date in months. I won't get pregnant. I always have safe sex." She turned her head to look at him, one eyebrow raised.

"Me too," he groaned. "In fact, I haven't had any sex for quite a while."

"Really? The hot hunky hockey player with all kinds of women after him?"

"I don't have women after me," he muttered.

Her hand reached back and slid over his hip. "I don't believe that. But never mind that. Fuck me, Tag."

She didn't need to ask twice. With another ragged groan he pushed inside, into the sweetest, hottest pussy. "Oh yeah."

She made hot little sex sounds as he filled her, pumped into her, her hands holding on tightly to the back of the seat. "Oh god, that's so good," she moaned. "So good."

He stroked her butt cheeks, so soft, played a little between them as he had the night before, teasing her puckered little entrance. "I want to fuck you here, Kyla," he muttered. He heard her sharp intake of breath. "Sometime. Maybe tonight." A moan fell from her lips. "Oh yeah. Touch yourself, Kyla. I'm gonna come fast, I've been hard all day thinking about this."

She slid her hand down to her clit and rubbed. "I like that. You being hard all day thinking about me."

"I can't stop thinking about you." The words slipped out before he could censor them. "Ah, hell..." He moved faster, his body bent over hers. He found her breasts and cupped them, squeezed them gently, tugged at her nipples. Then he wrapped his arms around her. She gave a soft cry and her pussy rippled around him.

Sensation climbed, then heat exploded inside him and flowed into her body. He bent over her and sank his teeth into her neck as their bodies shuddered together in a wild and violent climax.

"Holy shit," he gasped moments later. His thighs quivered. Sweat dripped from his forehead and he swiped an arm across it before slowly withdrawing from her body. He collapsed onto the seat beside her, the vinyl hot under his ass, and reached for her hand. She too fell onto the seat, and, half sitting, half lying, they stayed there holding hands, the softly rocking boat echoing the lingering pulses of ecstasy in his body, lulling his sated mind and body to near sleep in the hot sun.

"Now I can say I've had sex in a boat," Kyla murmured.

He smiled without opening his eyes. "Me too."

"Like you've never done this before."

"I haven't. And seriously, Kyla...about all those girls...there aren't any."

"A couple of years ago I heard you might be getting married."

He lifted his head and looked at her. "You heard that, huh." He stared past her out at the never-ending surface of the water, stretching all the way to the horizon, pure and blue. "Well, I thought I might be getting married too. It didn't work out."

"Why?"

"Let's eat lunch."

"You brought lunch?" She sat up and reached for her bathing suit. He plucked it out of her hand. "Hey!"

"Stay naked a little longer. This is seriously sexy."

She grinned. "Fine. But I can't believe you remembered food, but not condoms."

"I can't believe it either. Let's move up front." He spread out a blanket and they reclined on it in the sun. He reached into a small cooler bag. "Pastrami on rye. Lemonade. And…" He pulled a bag of potato chips from a plastic grocery bag. "Old Dutch potato chips. You have no idea how much I miss these living down in the States."

"Well, there's one more benefit of being back home."

"Definitely."

"So tell me why you didn't get married."

Damn. She wasn't going to let that go. He sighed. "Her name was Jovannah."

"She's from Phoenix?"

"Yeah. She manages a clothing store."

"Mmm."

He looked at her. "I know what you're thinking."

"No, you don't."

"Yes, I do. And you're right."

She laughed and picked up the bottle of lemonade. "Blonde bimbo with big boobs? Really? I'm right?"

He couldn't help it, he laughed too. Maybe Jovannah wasn't such a sore spot any more. "She wasn't really a bimbo. But definitely not as smart as you."

She tossed her hair back and took a bite of her sandwich.

"We were together a couple of years. I thought it was pretty serious. Then I had that knee injury…don't know if you heard about that."

"I did." Her eyes regarded him solemnly, attentively. All her focused attention on him made his chest go hot.

"I had to have surgery. I…well, it was stupid, the surgery went fine, but I was a little freaked out about it and worried that my hockey career was over." He bent his head and studied the potato chip in his hand. "I don't know what I'd do if that happened."

She didn't say anything.

"So," he continued. "I guess that kind of freaked Jovannah out too. Because it turned out my career was just as important to her as it is to me. In fact, more important than *I* was. She screwed around on me with another guy on the team. I guess she was making sure she had a backup plan if I ended up done playing hockey."

"Bitch."

He lifted his head. She met his eyes and she wasn't even smiling.

"Yeah." He tipped the lemonade bottle up to drink deeply. "It was hard because I felt stupid. I should've known that's what she wanted. I learned that lesson a long time ago."

"What lesson?"

"That women were only interested in me because of what I do for a living."

After two seconds of silence, she burst out laughing.

He frowned. "What?"

"That's not why women are interested in you! Are you kidding me?"

"No." His frown deepened.

She leaned forward, now apparently oblivious to her lovely nudity. "You're smart, gorgeous, funny. You're fair-minded and ethical and loyal and trustworthy. Yeah, you're...um...gorgeous... and super talented, but you've apparently never let that change who you are inside. *Those* are the reasons you have women all over you."

He stared at her, the heat in his chest becoming a swelling softness. "Ah..." For a moment he had a weird sensation, like being high, like he was floating out of his body and then plummeting back to earth.

"And you have mustard on your chin." One corner of her mouth lifted.

He grinned and swiped at his chin.

CHAPTER 11

"How was the fishing?"

Tag shot his mom a glance. "Uh. Not good. Didn't catch a thing."

"Really. That's too bad. I was thinking we'd have fish for dinner tonight."

"Sorry." He turned away from his mom in the kitchen to grab a beer from the fridge. "Guess it's burgers instead. Want me to help?"

He thought he heard his mom chuckle. "No, that's okay. Go out on the deck with your brothers. You could start the barbecue, though, and clean the grill."

So he did that. Logan, Matt and Jase were all already out there with beers in hand. He pushed the starter on the gas barbecue and closed the lid to let it heat up before he took the brush and scrubbed the grills. He leaned against the railing and took a big pull of his beer.

"Can't believe you didn't catch a single fish," Logan said.

Tag narrowed his eyes, then shrugged. "Not my lucky day."

When it came to fish. When it came to getting lucky...holy fuck, he and Kyla had definitely had a good afternoon. His groin tightened. He couldn't wait for tonight when she'd hopefully come to the tent again.

"So." Tag turned his gaze to Jase. "When are you getting a paternity test done?"

Jase's face tightened. He looked at his beer bottle. "I will."

"Damn right you will. I asked when?"

Jase rubbed his forehead. "When the baby's born."

"Why not before?"

"I, uh, didn't know you can do that."

"Yep." Tag drank more of the icy beer. "You can. I bet we can go do a Google search and find a Chicago clinic that would do it. You'd have to get Brianne there. Think she'd go?"

"How the hell do you know this?"

Tag shrugged. "Everyone knows that."

"I didn't," Logan said. "But then I never knocked a chick up."

"Neither have I!" Tag protested.

Jase sighed. "We used birth control. It was an accident."

"It's fucked up, man," Tag said, but tried to inject sympathy into his voice. Yeah, accidents happened. "Maybe you should also talk to a lawyer."

"What? Why?"

"If she refuses to go for a DNA test, there's probably a way you can legally make her. Especially if she claims you're the father. Hey, we could ask Kyla about it. She's a lawyer."

"Christ no, I'm not gonna talk to Kyla about it. Anyway. I don't think she specializes in that kind of stuff."

Tag lifted a shoulder. "Just want to make sure you're being smart about this, little brother."

Jase shook his head slowly and let out a long breath. "Yeah, I know what I have to do. Don't worry. I will."

"Okay, good. So. Who's getting their ass kicked at poker tonight?"

"What are you doing?"

Kyla's head snapped up, standing in her bedroom the next morning. She thrust her BlackBerry behind her back and stared at Tag. "What?"

He advanced on her, hand outstretched. "Give me the phone."

"What? No."

"Yes." He wiggled his fingers.

She took a step back and glared at him. "I'm not giving you my phone."

"You're on vacation. Hand it over."

She'd managed to last until Tuesday before turning her phone on, wondering what was happening at the office. She'd thought no one was around when she snuck into the bedroom where she had it plugged in charging. How the hell had Tag found her? "I'm just quickly checking emails."

"No. You're not."

He reached around behind her, his arms long. She tried to get away from him, but the room was small and she bumped into the dresser. "Tag!"

He grinned, crowding his big body up against hers and easily confiscating the device. He held it up. "I'll keep this for the rest of the week."

"No! You can't! Not my BlackBerry."

"Crackberry, apparently. Come on, babe. You've admitted how stressed you've been and how much you need some down time. They'll survive without you at work."

She pouted and crossed her arms. "I know they will." Then she sighed. "You're right."

"Come on. I'm going for a run. Come with me before it gets too hot."

"It's already too hot."

He laughed. "It's only twenty degrees. Come on. I'm going to change. I'll meet you out front in ten minutes."

"Leave my phone here. I promise I won't look at it."

Smiling, he shook his head. "No way, Mac. I'll give this back to you later this week."

"Grrrrr." She dropped her arms, hands curled into fists. "Fine." She tossed her hair back. "I can survive. I'm not addicted to it."

"Uh huh. Sure. See you in ten."

She scrunched her face up in frustration as he left, closing the bedroom door behind him. "Argh!" Then she blew out a breath and moved to the dresser. She pulled out a pair of shorts, her sports bra and a loose tank top. She wasn't even sure why she'd packed this stuff, except maybe she'd had the idea she should get some exercise while she was on vacation. She kicked off her flip flops and pulled on a pair of little white athletic socks then pushed her feet into rarely-worn Nikes.

She brushed her hair back and fastened it into a pony tail. She surveyed her face in the mirror. Damn. She already looked better. A few days of sun and relaxation had tanned her skin a little, and the tightness around her eyes and mouth had relaxed.

The sex might have something to do with it too.

Eeep. She was having hot, sweaty sex with Tag Heller. Her belly did a little flip and she pressed a hand there.

And now she was going for a run with him. This felt like her younger days when she'd chased the boys around. Now he'd invited her. Just her.

She jogged outside and found him on the road stretching his quads. Damn, he was gorgeous. He too had gotten tanned and his flexing muscles made her mouth water. She'd had her hands all over those muscles. Her insides quivered.

"I'm here." She set her hands on her hips. "Let's get on with my humiliation."

He grinned. "It won't be that bad."

They started out at an easy pace, though she was sure Tag was actually having a hard time moving that slowly. It did feel good to move like this and the scenery was lovely. Not just Tag. He was easy on the eyes, but the trees and shrubbery and wildflowers were pretty too. Soon they had left the small town of Crystal Beach and were running along a country gravel road, their feet crunching the stones beneath.

Sweat soon ran down her face, her chest, between her breasts.

"What did you do with my phone?"

"As if I'd tell you that."

"Seriously, I should check email."

"Seriously, you should not."

She shook her head, a smile tugging at her lips. "You are so damn bossy."

"Yep."

Tag made them turn around and go back before she was ready. "Better not to overdo it the first time," he said.

"I'm fine." But he was probably right again, dammit. She was still a little sore from water skiing. She didn't want to be laid up for the rest of the week because of this.

"You gonna make it back to the cottage?"

She frowned at him as she ran beside him. He was sweating, yeah, but seemed to be barely out of breath. "Of course. In fact, I'll race you."

She took off at a sprint, but immediately cursed her damn competitiveness. She was winded and her legs were tired and there was no way in hell she could beat him.

His feet pounded along behind her and she was pretty sure she heard a low laugh over her own loud breathing. Her lungs burned but she pushed herself as hard as she could. She was almost at the cottage when he leisurely passed her, slowing to a stop with hands on hips and walking back toward hers.

"Wipe that shit eating grin off your face," she panted.

He burst out laughing. "Baby, you never could keep up with us." But the kiss her laid on her mouth made up for his teasing reminder. "But I love how you try."

She glanced wildly around but nobody else was near to see him kiss her. "Don't do that!"

His grin stayed in place. "It's fine."

"I need a shower."

"Or a swim. Meet me at the beach."

"What is this? Boot camp?"

He laughed again. "Come on. The water will feel great. You can just dog paddle around if you want. Or float on your back."

Again, he was right. She longed to just run down to the beach and throw herself fin the lake. "I'll see you there."

Lungs still straining, dripping sweat, she walked into the cottage. Mom was making lunch in the kitchen.

"Whoa." Mom surveyed her. "What were you doing?"

"Tag made me go for a run with him." She scowled. "He seems to think it's his job to get me in shape."

Mom laughed.

"Where's everyone else?"

"Dad and Doug are golfing. The others are at the beach, I think."

"That's where I'm headed. Just need to change."

She walked into the bedroom she shared with Emily and stripped off her soaked clothing. Ugh. She probably reeked of sweat.

But damn, it did feel good.

She pulled on a swimsuit, this time a pink flowered one, slipped on flip flops and grabbed a beach towel from the cupboard in the hall.

"Lunch will be ready in about fifteen minutes," Mom called as she crossed the living room to the doors to the deck. "Laura's bringing potato salad over. Tell the others."

"Okay."

She skipped down to the beach. The voices of the others reached her as she neared the water, Emily's scream before a loud splash as someone—her uncle or one of her adopted "Heller uncles" probably—threw her in the water. Laughter ensued and Kyla's heart warmed.

Tag was already there, laughing as Emily begged Michael to toss her in the air again. He grinned and lifted her onto his shoulders. He caught Kyla's eye as she dropped her towel on the sand

and waded into the water. She smiled back at him, heat rising inside her and not from the run.

She didn't hesitate to enter the water this time, her skin overheated. She ran in and as soon as she was deep enough she dove in. It felt so delicious and cool, washing away the sweat. She tried to ignore Tag's scorching gaze on her when she surfaced and swiped water off her face.

Jessica and Scott were sitting on the beach with the baby, and Remi and Jase were playing together in the water. Matt and Logan were throwing a football back and forth again.

God, she loved these people.

"Apparently we're all having lunch at our place," she told the others, sliding into a slow backstroke. "Mom said lunch will be ready soon."

"I'm starving." Tag swam near her. Then her ankle was seized in a strong grip and she was pulled under the water.

Damn him. They'd done this to her so many times as kids. She held her breath, knowing he wouldn't keep her under long. When he released her, she shoved up and out of the water and gave his big chest a push. "Asshole!"

Oops. She made a face and glanced at Emily.

"Watch your language there, Auntie Kyla." Tag gave her a wicked grin.

After lunch, Jessica put Caleb down for a nap. "Hey Mom," Kyla said. "Would you look after Caleb and Emily while Jess, Remi and I go for a walk?"

"Of course."

"I'll stay and help," Laura said.

Kyla looked at Remi and Jessica. "If you're interested? I thought it would be nice to have some girl time to get to know each other better."

Obviously she already knew Jessica, but neither of them knew

114

Remi, and she wanted to make Remi feel more at ease, now knowing that Remi was feeling a little intimidated by the families.

"That would be nice," Remi said, with a grateful smile.

"Yes!" Jessica agreed and jumped up. "Let's go."

"I thought we could walk along the beach. I need to keep moving." Kyla rubbed her butt. "After that run, if I sit still, my muscles might seize up and I'll never move again."

"I need to work out more," Remi said as they crossed the grass toward the lake. "I used to take Taekwondo with my brother and sister, but when they quit, I did too."

"That's cool. I should do some kind of martial art."

"I have to get back to it, too," Jessica said. "I finally lost the baby weight but my stomach muscles still feel like jelly."

"You look great," Kyla said.

"Aw, thank you. Breastfeeding burns a gazillion calories. I freakin' love being able to eat whatever I want and lose weight."

"So jealous."

"As if you need to worry," Jessica gave her a look. "You've lost weight since I last saw you."

"I know. And not on purpose." Kyla blew out a breath. "Mom keeps bugging me that I'm too thin." She frowned. "And then Tag makes me run twenty miles."

Jessica and Remi laughed. "Twenty miles?"

Kyla grinned. "Okay, slight exaggeration. If we ran two miles, I'd be surprised. He's running again right now. Anyhoo, I guess the running is good for me."

"Sure it is." Jessica kicked a wave. "Scott says you might be made partner soon."

"I'm hoping. I think."

"You're not sure now?"

Kyla sighed. "I don't know. I was talking to…I mean, I've been thinking about it and…I've worked so hard for it. I want it so badly. But maybe I need a little more in my life than just work."

"I've been thinking that too," Remi said. "It's not my career that I'm so obsessed with, but my family." She told them about her

115

younger brother and sister leaving home after she'd raised them following their parents' death. "So I've been spending a lot more time working, but really I need to be doing more things for myself."

"You raised your younger siblings?" Kyla gazed at Remi. "Wow."

Remi shrugged. "Had no choice. I'm not sure how well I did at it. Actually, Jase has been giving me great advice lately."

"Jase? Mr. Fun?"

Remi laughed. "Yeah. You know, he's actually pretty mature."

"Ahem." Jessica chuckled. "Let's not talk about head."

They all burst out laughing.

"Seriously," Remi said, still grinning. "He is helping me."

"How are you dealing with this baby thing?" Jessica asked. "With Jase's ex?"

Kyla sensed Remi's tension. "I hate it," she said. "It almost broke us up."

"Oh no." Jessica's eyes shone with sympathy.

"Yeah. So, it's shitty. But it is what it is and we'll deal with it."

"I'm still impressed that you raised your brother and sister. That had to be hard."

"Sometimes it was, but I love them. They make me crazy but I'm trying to let go now they're adults."

"I like seeing you and Jase together," Kyla said. "He seems so happy. I have a soft spot for him in my heart."

"Thanks, Kyla." Remi sent her a sweet smile. "That means a lot. I know I got a little defensive of him the other day. I hate it when people make him feel like he's stupid."

Kyla bumped Remi's shoulder. "I don't think he's stupid, and I hated that too, when we were younger. I know he went through some tough times."

"Yeah, he told me about it. And I think you and Tag are a cute couple."

"What!" Jessica stopped walking and stared at them. "What?"

Kyla's body tightened. "No, no! We're not a couple!"

Remi just smirked. "Uh huh."

"No really." Kyla met Jessica's eyes.

"Scott would die," Jessica said slowly. "Seriously."

"I know." Kyla closed her eyes. "Don't worry. Not happening." She was lying.

When she opened her eyes to meet Jessica's again, she saw... concern. "Really?" the other woman asked. She tapped her chin. "I think Remi might be right, actually."

"No. It can't happen." Kyla bit her lip. "Oh god." She eyed the other girls. She'd already confessed her girlhood crush to Remi. She couldn't let on what had happened since then. "Do not say anything to anyone."

They exchanged glances, then regarded her solemnly. Remi held up a hand. "Not a word."

Kyla tipped her head. No. She couldn't take a chance and confess to them what had been going on. Remi would for sure tell Jase, and Jessica would tell Scott. They *had* to tell their men, right? But wow...she really felt like sharing, getting some girl perspective on things. But these had to be the two worst women in the world to confide in. Or maybe not...god, she was so confused.

"I've been sneaking down to his tent at night." The words rushed out of her.

After a couple of beats of silence, Remi gave a light laugh. "I knew it!"

"Holy shit." Jessica grinned. "Good for you."

Kyla bit her lip. "It doesn't mean anything."

They both nodded.

"You said you wanted to do him," Remi said. "You go girl!"

Jessica bit her lip. "Okay, I have to ask...how was it?"

"Fucking amazing." Kyla sucked in a long breath and let it out. She dropped to sit on the sand and wrapped her arms around her knees. "Just...wow. But you know...I'm a little worried about it."

"Why?" They both sat too. A seagull cried above them, a white arc against the blue sky.

"The whole family thing. Plus...I don't know. We agreed, it

would just be this week, and it's just sex. We go back to Winnipeg next week, and it's all over."

"But why?" Remi's forehead creased.

"Just…I have a demanding job. So does Tag right now. Neither of us has time. And our families would freak out."

"I don't know." Jessica pursed her lips. "They might be okay with it."

"Yeah, and then what happens when things end? Because most guys get fed up with my long hours pretty quick. It could wreck the friendship between Mom and Dad and Laura and Doug forever. And they'd all hate me."

To her surprise, Remi reached out and gave her forearm a quick rub. "You shouldn't think that. I don't think Laura and Doug could ever hate you."

"Really?" Kyla sighed. "Well, I'm not willing to find out. And this is crazy talk anyway, because I don't think Tag wants to find out that either. Like I said, we both agreed on what this is." She bit her lip to stop her grin, but then it broke free. "But what it is, is freakin' hot."

They both smiled back at her. "Awesome!"

"I still almost can't believe it." She gave them a wry smile. "I had such a crush on him when I was a kid." She frowned and held up a finger. "You can't tell *anyone* that."

They both shook their heads.

Kyla fell back onto the sand and stared up at puffy white clouds drifting across the sky. "This is so beautiful."

"It really is."

"You need to come visit us in Chicago," Remi said. "That would be fun."

Kyla turned her head and looked at her new friend. "It really would. I've never been to Chicago, but I've always wanted to go there." She grinned. "I like you, Remi."

"I like you too."

"Oh for eff sake." Jessica flicked sand at them. "I wanna be part of this lovin'."

118

"You know I love you, Jess." Kyla grinned at her sister-in-law. "And admire you for putting up with my brother."

"Ha."

An expanding warmth rose up inside Kyla and she relaxed even more. "This is a nice day."

"I need to get back to feed Caleb."

"Yeah. Let's head back. I want to hug my niece and nephew." Kyla jumped to her feet and swiped sand off the back of her shorts.

When they got back to the cottage, Tag and Scott were sitting on the MacIntosh deck with beers in hand, baby Caleb now sleeping in the crook of Scott's arm, the two men deep in conversation. The girls paused below the deck.

"Look at that," Jessica whispered.

Kyla's heart squeezed. Her brother looked so comfortable with the baby in his arm, and Tag was nodding at something Scott had said. It was so amazing to see the two old friends connecting like this. Their lives had changed since they were childhood buddies, but she loved that there was still that friendship between them.

"I love that," she whispered back.

Jessica squeezed her hand and they shared an understanding look.

This was what this week was about. Kyla was so glad she'd come. Reconnecting with friends and family—and making new connections—was important. They were all so busy but times like these were precious.

CHAPTER 12

Tag watched Kyla patting baby Caleb's back, holding him on her shoulder. Caleb had just been fed and Jessica was now cutting up Emily's hot dog. Kyla looked...good with that baby. Caleb let out a belch and Kyla grinned. "Attaboy."

She met his eyes, still smiling, and he smiled back at her.

"I don't want my hot dog cut up in wittow pieces." Emily pouted and folded her arms. "Want it in a bun, like Kywa."

Kyla's eyebrows raised. She wandered over to the counter. "What if you cut it in half lengthwise? And put it in a bun."

Jessica sighed. "Of course. Now what do I do with this one?"

Tag walked over and stretched out a hand. "I'll eat it. I don't care if it's in little pieces."

With a smile, Jessica hand him the plate and he wolfed down one more wiener after having just had three for lunch, although those ones had been in big sesame–seed topped rolls loaded with ketchup, mustard and relish.

He wanted more potato chips too, but Jessica had put out platters of vegetables and hidden the potato chips from Emily's view. The sacrifices you had to make for kids.

Kyla shifted Caleb in her arms, cradling him now as his eyes drifted shut. She smiled down at him with a tender expression that tugged at Tag's heart. "How about when this little dude is down you and I have some girl time?" she said to Emily. "Your mom and dad said they wanted to go into town and look around."

"What will we do?" Emily looked up from her hot dog.

"Hmm. I don't know. I saw a beautiful castle in our room I've been wanting to play with. You could show it to me."

Emily nodded vigorously. "Okay."

Kyla gently bounced Caleb as she strolled back and forth. "I think he's asleep. Should I go put him down?"

"Thank you, Kyla." Jessica wiped ketchup from Emily's small face.

Tag followed along, he didn't know why, and watched her set the sleeping baby into the little bassinette they'd set up in Jessica and Scott's room, carefully laying him on his back.

She straightened and started to see him watching. "What?"

He shrugged. "You're cute."

She gave him a look. "Uh huh."

"And sexy."

"Hush."

He grinned. "I said it quietly. No one's around."

The others were all out on the deck having just finished lunch.

"So you're playing with Emily this afternoon, huh. No fishing trip?"

"People are starting to wonder why we're not catching any fish."

Tag laughed. He was pretty sure they knew exactly why they weren't catching any fish, but he wasn't going to embarrass her by telling her that. There'd been a few awkward moments with the family, and it was getting harder and harder to keep his hands off her when they were around.

"Ah well, no fishing. Logan wants to ski again this afternoon. So we'll go do that, while Scott and Jessica go into town."

He left her and headed out to the MacIntosh deck. A while later, he and his brothers and Michael jumped in the boat and cruised out onto the lake. The water was super calm and perfect for skiing, so they all took a few turns. Without any of the girls there, they could try all the crazy stunts they wanted without scaring anyone. Remi and Jessica, and yes even Kyla, had freaked out when he'd tried to do tricks.

Then it happened—he was just skiing along, maybe a little cocky, when his slalom ski caught an edge and flipped him ass over head, and his thumb got caught in the tow rope. The hard yank had pain searing up his arm as he was being briefly dragged through the water. He swallowed lake water, fought for breath, and somehow managed to free his thumb. He burst to the surfacing, coughing and gasping, his hand throbbing. "Fuck!" he managed to yell.

Matt had been spotting and had called for Jase to turn the boat around. They were racing back toward him. He kicked his feet to tread water. "Jesus fucking Christ motherfucking hell."

"What the hell? You okay?" Jase cut the motor and the boat slid up beside them. Matt was pulling in the tow rope.

"Motherfucker," Tag said again, holding his injured hand. "Caught my thumb in the tow rope. I think it's still attached, but Jesus fucking Christ."

Matt reached down and held Tag back into the boat where he collapsed, dripping, onto the one of the hot vinyl seats.

"Let's have a look." Logan moved over.

Tag sucked in a breath as they all studied his thumb.

Logan pressed the sides of his thumb gently between his fingers. "That hurt?"

"No."

Logan carefully moved the joints and Tag gritted his teeth. "Fuck!"

"Hmm." Logan grimaced. "I don't think it's broken but you should probably get it x-rayed."

"Shit."

"Heading back." Jase put the boat in gear and took off with a roar. In a few minutes, they were at the dock. Tag was pissed off at himself and his hand was throbbing. Godammit, this shouldn't have happened.

Back at the cottage, Mom jumped to attention when he walked in holding his hand and clearly in pain. "What happened?"

"Caught my thumb in the tow rope when I went down."

"Let's have a look."

"Jesus. Now you." He let his mom examine him. "Logan says I need to get it x-rayed."

"I agree. Sit down and don't move."

He lowered himself to a chair at the big round dining table. Mom hustled into the kitchen and returned with a small plastic ice pack that she gently eased onto his thumb.

"I'm going to splint it." She moved way and pulled open a drawer. "Ha. Thought we had these. Logan, can you bring the first aid kit from the bathroom?"

"Sure."

"I'll have to go all the way back to Winnipeg for an x-ray." Tag scowled at the ice pack.

"Yeah. You should call Harv," Jase said, referring to the head trainer of the Jets. "He'll tell you what to do. They can probably get one of the team doctors to see you fast."

Tag sighed and held out his other hand. "Can you get my phone? It's charging over there."

Jase handed him his phone and while his mom splinted his thumb with two Popsicle sticks and some tape, he called Harv and told him what had happened. "Yeah, I'll come in," he agreed reluctantly. "Be there in just over an hour."

He ended the call. "He's gonna call Dr. Warren. He's an orthopedic surgeon."

"He's good," Mom said. "Keep the ice on it."

"How'm I gonna drive with an ice pack on it?"

"You're not driving," she said firmly.

"I'll take you," Logan spoke up. "No problem."

"Great." Tag sighed. "Let me change."

Kyla appeared at the sliding doors onto the deck, looking sexy in short shorts and a tank top that said, "Lawyers do it legally". "Hey guys," she said through the screen, then slid it open and stepped inside. "Mom wants to know…*what happened*?"

"Hurt my thumb." Jase rose to his feet, waving the splinted digit. "Skiing."

She blinked and he sensed that she wanted to rush over. "Is it broken?"

"Don't think so, but Logan's taking me back to Winnipeg to get it x-rayed."

"Even if it's just dislocated, you want to make sure it's back in proper position," Mom said. "You don't want to fool around."

"I know, I know. What a pain in the ass, though."

Kyla nibbled her bottom lip. "You were probably showing off, weren't you."

Tag had to laugh. "Actually no. It was so fucking stupid, I was just skiing along, caught the edge of my ski somehow…I don't even know how it happened." He read the concern in her eyes, her brows sloped downward. "I'll be fine."

"What if it's broken? Will that impact the start of the season?"

Fuck. He'd already thought that. "I guess we'll see. I gotta change out of my board shorts. Back in a flash, Lo."

He hurried to the bedroom and changed out of his nearly-dry shorts, with some difficulty maneuvering into a pair of cargo shorts and a T-shirt. "Who knew opposable thumbs were so valuable," he said dryly when he returned.

"Take this." Mom shoved two pills at him.

"I'm fine, Mom."

"I know you're a big tough guy, but they're an anti-inflammatory. If you've sprained or strained something, they'll help."

He tossed them in his mouth and took the bottle of water she handed him to drink. "Okay, done. Let's go." He caught Kyla's eye where she still stood in the doorway, now twisting her fingers together. He wanted to go over and kiss her and reassure her he was fine, but had to satisfy himself with a wink. "Back in a while."

She nodded.

124

~

Three hours later, he and Logan were back. Everyone was over at the MacIntosh cottage cleaning up after dinner. They'd apparently barbecued steaks and it smelled fucking amazing. His stomach growled. "Please tell me you saved us a steak," he demanded, walking in.

They all looked up at him.

"What? I'm starving."

"I told you we could've gone through the drive through," Logan said. "I was starving an hour ago."

"How's your thumb? Is it broken?" Mom started toward him, tossing the dish towel over her shoulder.

"Not broken. Probably dislocated it, but it's fine. Strained some ligaments." He grinned at her. "You did the exact right thing—ice, splint, ibuprofen."

"Of course I did the right thing." She huffed. "I've treated more than my fair share of injuries over the years."

"Four to six weeks, should be good. Won't even impact training camp."

His eyes sought out Kyla and she gave him a beaming smile of relief.

She cared.

Damn. So did he.

"And yes, we saved steaks for you. I'll warm them up."

"I can do it," Tag said.

Kyla pulled two clean plates out of a cupboard. "I'll get you guys some potatoes and veggies. There's lots left."

When he was sitting at the table with a thick juicy steak in front of him, he picked up his knife and fork and discovered he couldn't cut the damn thing. He stared at it.

He heard a soft sigh, then Kyla plucked his cutlery from his hands. "Here."

She cut the steak into bite-size pieces for him.

"Hmm. I could get used to this."

"Kyla, will you cut my steak too?" Logan asked.

She laughed. "Want me to break your fingers?" She patted his shoulder and he laughed.

For some reason, tonight Tag felt even more urgently the need to get Kyla alone. This fucking sucked that they had to pretend they didn't give a shit, when he wanted some sympathy kisses and also wanted to reassure her that he was fine.

Kyla lay in her bed in her shorts and hoodie, wide eyed and staring at the bottom of the top bunk, waiting for everyone else to fall asleep. Tag had scared the crap out of her earlier.

When she'd walked in and seen him in pain, his hand all bandaged up, she'd felt a visceral reaction down low inside her... almost like she was feeling his pain. She'd so wanted to go to him and comfort him and make sure he was okay. She'd wanted to speak up and offer to drive him back to the city, but she'd bit her lip.

Now, she still wanted to see him. Apparently he was fine, but still...she sucked in a long breath and let it out.

Okay. She threw back the covers, then straightened them, shoving a pillow under them as she had every night in case someone peeked in on Emily, then tip-toed out of the cottage.

An owl hooted in a distant tree as she skipped across the grass to the tent. The lamp was still on, making the tent glow. She slipped inside.

Tag was lying on the sleeping bag, reading on a tablet, holding it up with his good hand. "Hey, baby." He tossed the tablet aside and rolled to face her.

She pounced on him, careful of his thumb though. "Are you really okay?"

He grinned. "I really am."

She laid kisses all over his face. "I was scared."

"Minor injury, Mac. I've had way worse."

"God." She kissed his lips. "I know you have. But still…"

"I like the sympathy." He caught her and rolled her under him.

"Be careful!"

"I'm fine." Now he kissed her, slow and sensuous, his lips warm and firm and coaxing. "Open your mouth for me."

She parted her lips and his tongue slid inside, stroking against hers. A rush of red-hot heat centered between her legs and she moaned. Her fingers curled around the back of his neck and he kissed her again and again, long, deep wet kisses that had her burning up with feverish need.

He lifted his head to smile down at her. The lamplight gilded his brown hair, his dark eyes in shadows, the carved shape of his cheekbones and mouth so beautiful. "I should've played the injury card sooner."

She smiled back at him, her fingertips brushing over his short hair. "You're a bad boy."

"You know it." And he lowered his head to suck on the skin on the side of her neck. Shivers cascaded down her body, her muscles tightening and nerve endings tingling everywhere. Her toes curled into the sleeping bag. "And you love it." He ran his tongue over the spot he'd just love-bitten. "Let's be bad together."

The rest of the week passed quickly, with time spent talking to her mom and dad and to her brothers, getting to know her little niece better, holding and playing with baby Caleb.

And she spent every night in the tent with Tag.

The hardest times were when she and Tag were together with their families. She tried her best to ignore Tag despite the heated haze of lust that surrounded her every time he was near. And sometimes when he wasn't. It was nearly impossible. Their gazes would catch and hold, sparks sizzling through her veins every time, her stomach doing a slow roll of lust, heat expanding around them. She'd thought they were doing a good job of hiding it though, even the sneaking into the tent every night, until Saturday afternoon, the day before she was supposed to leave, when she ended up in the Heller kitchen alone with Laura, helping prepare dinner to barbecue that night. Remi'd been helping them, but had just gone to buy more wine.

"Okay, I have to ask you something," Laura said. "It's kind of personal, but don't be upset."

Kyla's stomach tightened. What was this about?

Laura smiled at her. "You and Tag…is something going on between you?"

Heat swept from Kyla's chest to her face and she knew she was blushing. Dammit. "Er…why do you ask that?"

"Just a feeling I have. You two have been spending a lot of time together this week."

"Um…well, we all have."

"I haven't seen you disappear with Logan or Matt in the boat for hours to go fishing. And then come home with no fish. Or taking longs walks on the beach. Or…" Her smile deepened. "Come to think of it, I've never seen Tag actually lie on the beach. But he has this week. With you."

Kyla bit her lip and bent her head to the chicken breasts she was trimming, letting her hair fall over her face. She couldn't lie to Laura. Was Laura upset about this?

"You know I've always thought of you as the daughter I didn't have." Laura whisked up lemon juice and Dijon mustard for the marinade. She gave a little laugh. "Doug and I kept trying for a girl and look what we ended up with. Four boys."

Kyla lifted her head to give Laura a smile, her words making her chest feel warm. "You love your four boys."

"I do. But having you as almost part of the family was so nice. I liked having a girl around. Even though you wanted to be one of the boys."

Kyla gave a choked little laugh. "I tried. I don't think I ever really was."

"That's not a bad thing. Clearly Tag doesn't see you as one of the boys. Or even a little sister."

Kyla paused. "Does that bother you?" Her body tensed, waiting Laura's reply. She couldn't bear if Laura was angry about this.

"No!"

Kyla's gaze flew up to Laura's face.

"Not at all! I think it's wonderful." Laura studied her and Kyla's insides twisted. "I love you, Kyla, and if you and Tag…well, I'd love that too. So much."

Oh no. This was worse than Laura being upset. This was Laura getting the wrong idea and getting false hopes about something that was never going to happen. Kyla dropped the knife and slumped against the counter. "Oh. Well, I'm not sure how to say this but…neither Tag or I are looking for any kind of relationship."

"Oh." Laura's smile drooped a little. "I thought…"

What could she say? How could she make this better? How could she tell Tag's mom they were just having hot tent sex every night, naked public sex in boats and long make-out sessions on the beach when they could get a moment alone.

They were also having long talks, sharing hopes and fears, talking about their futures…but never a future together. Kyla's heart thudded slowly in her chest. "Laura. We're both adults. Whatever this is…it's going to end tomorrow when I head back to Winnipeg and…" Her voice got stuck, her throat suddenly thick and swollen. "And…" To her horror, tears sprang to her eyes. She met Laura's gaze with an appalled silence.

"Oh no. Oh, Kyla." Laura immediately moved toward her and drew her in for a hug.

"I can't…touch you…chicken hands…" She'd just been handling raw chicken and couldn't touch anything. Laura gave a sniffly laugh and squeezed her, then drew back. She touched Kyla's cheek.

"Are you okay, Kyla?"

Kyla nodded. "Of course! I'm fine. I never cry! This is so stupid. I don't know what came over me."

Laura grabbed a tissue and dabbed at her wet cheeks for her. She opened her mouth to say something, then closed it. "You probably don't want to talk to me about it. I'm his mom. But you could talk to *your* mom. Or even Remi. She likes you and she's a very good listener."

"I don't need to talk to anyone."

"Or maybe you should talk to Tag about it."

Kyla's eyes widened and she shook her head. "No! There's nothing to talk about. We both knew what we were getting into…" Well, there. She'd pretty much just told Laura they'd been boinking their brains out all week. She swallowed. "We're just having fun, Laura."

Laura nodded. "Okay." But Kyla didn't miss the disappointment that crossed Laura's face.

Damn! She'd always thought their parents would be horrified if something like this happened. She'd never in a million years thought that maybe Laura *wanted* her and Tag to get together! Dear god, that was crazy.

Her insides churned as she returned to the chicken breasts, trying to focus on them.

Just then Remi returned from the store. "I'm back!" She set the bags of wine bottles on the dining table. "They don't have a big selection at that little store, but I got something anyway."

But Remi apparently had instincts as good as Laura's and she looked back and forth between Kyla and Laura as she unpacked the bags to put the wine if the fridge. Kyla forced a smile. "Great."

"How's the food coming? What can I do?"

"You can snap this asparagus," Laura said with a smile as bright and forced as Kyla's.

Damn.

CHAPTER 13

It was their last night all together. Kyla and Tag were both heading back to the city on Sunday. They both had work obligations they had to get back to. So the two families had planned a big barbecue on the MacIntosh deck.

After they'd cooked and drank wine and eaten, they all sat on the deck. A blanket of pale gray obscured the sky, meaning rain was likely coming, but the evening air was still soft and warm. Then Kyla looked up to see her dad climbing up on a chair. "Dad! What are you doing?"

"I'm making a speech."

She slouched back in her chair, waiting. She smiled and sipped her wine. Dad was used to public speaking in his role as CEO, often traveling all over the world to give business presentations, so had no reservations about standing on a chair in front of the family to make a speech.

"I just want to say a few words while we're all together," he began. "It doesn't happen very often any more, that all our kids can be home at the same time. Now our family is growing with Jessica, and grandchildren. The Heller family is growing too, with Remi here." He smiled at Remi. "And maybe I'm not supposed to mention it, everyone has been tiptoeing around this all week, but Doug and Laura are going to be grandparents too."

Everyone exchanged uneasy glances. Jase's ex-girlfriend's pregnancy wasn't something anyone felt very comfortable talking about. Trust Dad to put it out there.

"That's the truth, and even though it may not be ideal circumstances, I know Jase is going to be a great father and we'll have another little one running around here soon. That child will be as welcome here as any. Just wanted to you to know that, Jase and Remi."

They both nodded, Jase's mouth tight, Remi's eyes bright.

"You all know that our family's been through a rough time over the last year with Jenn's cancer diagnosis."

Another subject no one really wanted to talk about, another elephant on the deck, so to speak.

"So that just makes us extra grateful for this time together and for everything we have. " Dad paused to take a sip of his drink and Kyla suspected he was feeling a little emotional. "Having our whole family around us this week has been an incredible gift. That includes you Heller boys too," he added with a smile. "All of us— Doug and Laura, Jenn and I—are so proud of all you kids. Not kids any more. Grown adults, all of you successful and bright and happy. That means so much to us."

Kyla looked around. There was Tag, Logan and Jase, big hockey superstars, and Matt just drafted into the NLH in the first round. There was her brother, VP at a big bank, the one who'd given her parents their first grandchildren, and Michael the tech entrepreneur making money like crazy.

And her. She looked down at her drink. This would have been the perfect time to celebrate her making partner. Her stomach tightened. It wasn't a competition. She knew that. But she felt like the least successful of all of them in terms of her career.

Hell, her life overall wasn't any better. She'd sacrificed so much working for the partnership, she didn't have a husband or children or even a boyfriend. She sighed.

"So," her father finished. "We just want to thank all of you for making the effort to be here, even though some of you have other obligations. When it comes right down to it, family is the most important thing and we know we've raised all of you right at times like this. So let's drink a toast—to family."

That old guilt nudged her again, at the fact that she'd almost missed this. Kyla lifted her drink in the toast and smiled and caught Tag's eye. Heat speared through her again. Their eyes met and held and she gulped her wine. Family. She remembered the things they'd talked about this past week, his tough questions about her job and her future.

She was going back to work on Monday to resume that plan toward partner. But as that thought entered her head and nerves buzzed in her stomach, it was then she realized how incredibly different she'd felt this past week. How easy and relaxed she'd felt —no headaches, no sore neck, no stomach problems, no panic attacks. Well, just the one.

She'd laughed a lot, talked a lot, cooked and eaten and enjoyed food more than she had in a long time, exercised more than she had in years, swimming, water skiing, running with Tag. She'd had a lot of very hot sex, which had also probably been very therapeutic. She'd had fun. The idea of going back to her workaholic existence suddenly seemed less appealing.

Dad approached and smiled at her. "Hey, sweetpea."

"Nice speech, Dad."

"Thanks. I know it was hard for you to get up here this week. Just wanted you to know we appreciate it. Especially your mom. We worry about you."

She sighed. She'd heard this before. "I know. You don't need to. I'm determined to make partner, Dad. Don't worry, I'll live up to the rest of you some day."

He frowned and tipped his head. "That's not what I meant, sweet pea. I mean we worry that you focus too much on your work. You need to have a life." He paused. "I'm not sure how you got the idea that we expect that of you. I mean...you're an intelligent, talented woman. We know you're capable of doing whatever you want in this world. But we love you no matter what that is, Kyla. If you make partner, we'll be proud, sure. But if you don't, we'll still be proud. We just want you to be happy."

She opened her mouth to tell him she *was* happy, but couldn't say it. Because she was starting to realize…maybe she wasn't.

"I know I was away on business a lot," he continued. "But there were a lot of trips I cut short so I could be back for your piano recital or one of Scott or Michael's games. My bosses always knew that family came first."

She gazed up at her dad, remembering those times he'd rushed in the door just in time for her jazz band concert or a playoff game. There'd been things he missed, yeah, but looking back, she had to admit he'd made a big effort to be there for them as a dad. And had still managed to climb the corporate ladder.

"I don't think you know this, but I once turned down a promotion because it meant we would have to move to Germany."

"What!" She gaped at him.

"Your mom and I talked about it. We didn't want to uproot you and your brothers."

"But…wow."

"Family is most important. If you got the idea from me that career is most important, then…I am so sorry."

"It's not your fault I'm like this," she said, voice husky. "It's just me."

"Ambitious." He smiled, laying a hand on top of her head. "I understand that. Just make sure your priorities are straight. Need another drink?" He held up his empty glass.

"That's okay, I'm good."

Dad moved on and the conversation rose and fell around her, Remi's soft laugh, Tag's deep voice, Emily's non-stop chatter. Her eyes sought out Tag and watched him.

It was their last night together.

What had started as a week of fun, exploring the sexual attraction that had always been there between them, had turned into something that felt like a lot more. Maybe she shouldn't even go to his tent tonight. Her emotions were all close to the surface today. First she'd nearly burst into tears in front of Tag's mom, now Dad had almost made her cry again with his touching speech about family. Having sex with Tag always made her feel more, and tonight...that might not be a good idea.

He looked up and once again met her eyes, his lips quirking into a small smile, so warm, so sexy. Just for her. Her heart tilted crazily in her chest.

Much later, Tag lay in the tent, waiting for Kyla as he had every night for the past week. It was their last night. Thinking of all the things they'd done there made him realize he'd grown very fond of this tent.

Yeah, they'd tried out pretty much every kinky toy in his bag of tricks. Kyla'd proven sexually adventurous and surprisingly willing to let him take charge in bed. Submissive, but yet an active participant. They were a good match that way and he got hot all over just remembering everything they'd done.

They were a good match in other ways too, he had to admit. He liked being with her even when it wasn't late at night in the tent. They laughed at the same things, had that easy way of talking to each other about pretty much anything. Sometimes when they were in the big family group, someone would say something and he'd look at her and know, somehow, that she was thinking the same thing he was.

It had been a good week, but next week was back to reality.

He was excited about it. He smiled up into the tent, hands behind his head lying on the bed. He'd felt overwhelmed before he'd had this week up here, overwhelmed by all the new expectations of him, the pressure of it. But strangely enough, after talking to Kyla about it, and also after talking to her about her career, he'd realized—he loved it. He loved *playing* hockey, but he loved every-

135

thing about hockey—the business of it too. And he loved promoting it and talking about it to the whole world. It felt like contributing to the team and to the sport in a whole new way. Maybe he'd be good at it. He wanted to be.

So while this week had been great, he was looking forward to getting back to the city and jumping back into things.

A shadow appeared at the tent door and Kyla slipped in.

"Hey," she said quietly, fastening the door.

He watched her, as always fascinated by the graceful way she moved, her slender body, her long shiny hair and her alluring smile. She sat on the bed beside him and looked at him.

Oh-oh.

"I wasn't sure if I should come," she said.

"Why?"

"I don't know, exactly. I just thought…maybe it was better to leave things the way they were. I know we're both going to be thinking this is our last night and I don't want to make it into more than it is."

His gut clenched. He chose his words carefully. "We talked about this. We both felt the same."

"Yes. We did." She looked up at him and smiled, her white teeth gleaming in the dim tent. "So I'm here. For one last night. Better make it good, buddy."

He laughed. She constantly surprised him. "C'mere, Mac."

He pulled her down so she lay on top of him and she stretched out. He parted his legs so she fit between and she kissed him, one hand on his face, her hair falling down around them. He opened his mouth beneath hers, slid his tongue inside and wrapped his arms around her body, holding her tightly as they kissed. As always, just kissing her heated his blood and hardened his cock.

One hand slid into her hair and held her head as they kissed, long, wet kisses, and he gave himself up to it, the softness of her mouth, the feel of her breasts pressed against his chest. She moved on him in a sinuous little wriggle and he spread his legs wider for her, lifted his hips into her softness.

Damn she was sweet.

She bit softly at his lips, rubbed her nose against his and breathed in. His chest expanded with warmth and the rush of emotion made him roll her over, tucking her beneath him. Both still fully clothed, he sealed his mouth back over hers and pressed her down into the mattress. His teeth grazed her jaw and she trembled. His tongue dragged up the side of her neck and she moaned. Her hands grabbed at his back, tugged his shirt up until she found skin.

It was their last night together.

He wasn't supposed to think about that. He was just supposed to remember how much fun this week had been, how beautiful she was, how hot the sex had been. It was just sex.

He buried his face in the side of her neck and breathed in her scent, a scent he would never forget, spicy sweet and coconutty. Maybe she only smelled like that here at the lake from the sunscreen she used, but he loved it. He opened his mouth on the soft skin there and tasted her.

Her hands ran up and down his back and she made needy little noises deep in her throat. He lifted his head and raised his hand to her forehead, pushing her hair back, resting his hand there. Gazing down at her, he said, "You know how much I love foreplay."

"Yes," she breathed. "You're a god. A foreplay sex god."

He couldn't help the laugh her words tugged out of him. Jesus. "I'm just warning you, tonight's not about foreplay. I have to be inside you, Kyla, like now."

"Okay, yes, yes." She wriggled her hips against him again, sending flames shooting from his balls up his spine. He groaned.

He rose up to strip off her T-shirt, tonight a little black one that said, "Lawyers do it with appeal." He'd shaken his head in amusement earlier when he'd seen her in it. Now it was coming off.

She half sat so he could pull it over her head, her hair a wild tangle around her head once the shirt had dragged through it. Hot. He reached behind her to unfasten her bra. Another source of fascination, the underwear she wore beneath those saucy little T's and short shorts, all silky and sheer and lacy, in colors of bubble gum and peach and lemon.

She lifted her hips so he could pull off the little shorts and tiny thong panties. His heart raced in his chest and his dick throbbed. He bent his head to kiss each thigh, drew her scent inside him, kissed the patch of curls between her legs. He slipped his hand between them as he moved back over her. "Oh yeah. So wet."

He yanked his own T-shirt over his head, then stripped off his cargo shorts along with his briefs. With warm eyes and a sweet smile, she watched him as he moved back over her, supporting himself on his arms while he kissed her mouth again. Her hands came up to his waist.

More emotion rose inside him, surprising him, almost choking him, and then he was inside her, her sweet heat clasping him, her hips lifting to meet his. "Yes," she whispered. "God, yes. Tag. Fuck me."

Oh yeah. *Oh yeah*. He kissed her, then moved back onto his knees, spread wide. She raised her knees for him and he thrust in deeper still, so deep, fucking her deep. He curved his hands around her slender waist and held her, bracing her for each plunge of his cock inside her. Her breasts quivered, so soft and perfect. Her lips parted and she gazed back up at him with those beautiful dark eyes, full of something…

He closed his eyes, his heart stuttering. His breath dragged in and out of his lungs as pleasure poured through him with each stroke. And then he had to look at her again, to see her face even though what he saw there made his insides tremble.

Lots of times good sex made him feel like he was in love, and maybe he was, a little, with the woman he was with at the time, but it didn't usually last and the one time he'd let it, he'd ended up fucked over. He'd vowed that would never happen again, so sex was sex and that was all it was.

This was so much more than sex it made his heart hurt. But Christ, he couldn't go there again. With a long shredded groan, he fell over her and buried his face in the side of her neck, sucking her flesh so gently, licking her there, his arms around her head. Her fingernails bit into his back, scraped up and down, and every nerve ending ignited. They moved together perfectly in exquisite unison, their bodies fitting together flawlessly, the drag and pull of her pussy on his dick an almost unbearable sweetness. Tension coiled inside him, a twisting flame, and he gasped her name.

She urged him on with whispers and murmurs, her legs wrapped around his hips, rocking and clutching, and once more he lifted up to kiss her, his hand on her forehead, then he looked down at her. Her eyes glowed with unspoken emotion, a connection between them he could feel pulling them together. His chest clenched, his body tightened and he was gone, all the way gone, every thought in his head lost, just feeling, feeling her around him, her hands on him, feeling...love.

CHAPTER 14

It was harder saying good-bye to everyone than she'd expected. Kyla had gotten closer with Jessica and Remi, and with her niece and nephew, and it would be a long time before she saw them again.

"Christmas," Laura said. "Maybe everyone can come home for Christmas this year. Logan's in Minneapolis. Jase is in Chicago." She looked at Scott and Jessica.

"I don't know," Scott said slowly. "We'll see."

Kyla met Jessica's eyes and felt a little sting in the corners of her own. But she smiled and held out her arms for a hug. They squeezed each other. "Put lots of pictures of these kids on Facebook," Kyla whispered to her. "I want to see them growing up."

"We will."

She hugged Remi next, equally as tightly.

"Come to Chicago," Remi said again. "Any time. I'll show you around. We can go shopping, see a play…you'll love it. Maybe go to one of Jase's games."

Kyla nodded, still teary. "I want to do that. I'll be in touch."

Her hugs for Laura and Doug were less emotional, as she'd see them soon. Same with her own parents, and Michael, who she

140

just punched. Then she had to say good-bye to the Heller brothers.

She hugged Matt. "Work hard at school, buddy. I'm sure you're a big man on campus now you're a first round draft pick."

He laughed.

Then she embraced Jase. "Good luck," she said to him quietly. "And listen to your big brother about that test."

He smiled wryly and hugged her back.

"Also, I love Remi," she whispered to him. "Be good to her."

"I plan to."

She then gave Logan a squeeze. "When does training camp start?"

"Physicals are September eleventh."

"Good luck."

Then there was Tag. They looked at each other. She had to make this casual, with everyone else around, even though electricity arced between them. He reached for her and pulled her into a hug. His body vibrated with tension against hers as he held her briefly, his cheek brushing against her hair. "It's been good to see you again, Mac," he murmured.

Her throat swelled up thick and aching and she closed her eyes briefly, hugging him back. "You too," she managed to whisper, pulling away.

She made her smile bright and wide. Dad had put her suitcase in the trunk of her car, so she lifted a hand as she climbed into the driver's seat. The tears started sliding down her cheeks before she'd even reached the highway.

She brushed them fiercely away. She couldn't cry and drive. She needed to get control of her emotions so she could make it home alive.

She had the next hour to think. About Tag. About what had happened last night between them. She'd come so close to telling him she loved him and she didn't even know where the words had come from. They just seemed to rise up inside her, uncontrollable. It was ridiculous. She had no intention of falling in love or messing her plans up with a relationship. Guys expected too much—they wanted all her attention, didn't want her working sixteen hour days, expected her to be free on weekends.

Who the hell was she kidding? Who could blame them for that? Who wanted that kind of life forever? She wasn't stupid, but she'd definitely been blind. Or blinkered. Or stubborn. Whatever. The closer she got back to the city, the tighter her stomach got and the more her head began to ache from clenching her jaw.

She had time to think about her career and all the questions Tag had asked that she didn't want to answer. She had time to think about Dad's words to her, about family being first. The truth was, when she really thought about it, she hadn't been entirely happy for a while. And looking into the future, even if she did get what she wanted, which was making partner, she wasn't so sure now she'd be any happier. A heaviness filled her.

Her BlackBerry, plugged into the charger, chimed on the seat beside her. Tag had returned it to her that morning. It was against the law to talk on a cell phone while driving, so she just glanced at it. Then it chimed again. And again. Shit.

She grabbed the phone, hoping there weren't any RCMP cars out patrolling to see her, and swiped her thumb over the screen. Christ. A ton of missed calls, starting Wednesday. All from the office.

Thanks, Tag. Annoyance that he'd taken her phone from her buzzed inside her. But then she sighed. She'd had a wonderful, stress free week. Her job wasn't a matter of life and death. She tossed the phone down. What was she going to do about it now, on a Sunday evening?

But she found herself parking in the small loading zone outside the Richardson Building. She could run into the office and her car would be okay there on a Sunday night for a couple of hours.

She turned on the lights in her office and powered up her computer. She surveyed the folders and documents that had piled up in her week's absence.

Three hours later, she'd checked emails, found out what all

the calls were about, done some research and had solved the problem. Now she was ready for Monday morning. Sure she was.

Her condo felt empty and cold when she walked in even though she'd turned down the air conditioning before she'd left. She didn't bother with lights, just grabbed a pair of pajamas out of a drawer, washed her face and climbed into bed.

Alone.

For the first time in a week, she slept alone, her bed cold and empty, especially after last night, after the impassioned, heated way she and Tag had come together. She'd felt so cherished, so cared for, so free to be herself without judgment, only respect. Admiration and affection had emanated from the depths of his dark eyes as he watched her with steady eyes while they made love. She rolled, turning her face into her pillow and closing her eyes, an ache of longing spreading through her body. Tag.

Hell. If she needed an orgasm she could give that to herself. She slipped her hands under her shorts and between her legs. But it only took a few seconds to realize she wasn't in the least turned on. She just...missed him. She was in big trouble because she didn't need sex...she just needed Tag.

Tag and Jase left Twin Pines Country Club after finalizing some details for the charity golf tournament the four brothers were hosting the next day. They climbed into the Jeep Cherokee Tag had just bought a week ago and Tag reversed out of the parking spot.

"Looks like we're good to go," Jase said.

"Yeah."

"You did a lot of work on this."

"Yeah. You guys weren't here, so someone had to do it."

When Jase said nothing, Tag glanced sideways at him and caught his pissed off look. "What?"

"We couldn't get here any sooner, Logan or me. Matt was here and he said he helped."

"Yeah, he helped a little." Tag shrugged.

"What the hell's your problem?" Jase demanded as Tag pulled out onto Highway #1 just outside the Perimeter.

"I don't have a problem."

"Yeah, you do. You've been snarly all week, with everyone. Ever since we came back from the lake."

"Just got a lot on my mind. There's a lot of stuff going on with the team and this golf tournament."

"Yeah. And what else?"

Tag shot him an annoyed glance. "Nothing else."

"Are you pissed because you won't be able to golf?"

"I'll be able to golf. Lay off, all right?"

Thick silence filled the Jeep and Tag stabbed at the button for the radio. The music of Eminem filled the Jeep, the expensive sound system creating a deep booming bass. Jase reached over and cranked the volume down.

Tag glared at him again.

"What's bugging you?" Jase asked again.

"Nothing."

"Bullshit." Jase sighed. "Jesus. Are you really that pissed off that you had to do most of the work for this tournament?"

Tag sighed. "No."

"Okay, I'm gonna go out on a limb here. Does this have anything to do with Kyla?"

Tag's chest tightened. "Kyla? What the fuck? No."

"Huh." Jase paused. "Because we knew what was going on in that tent last week."

Tag's stomach jumped. "*Who knew?*"

Jase grinned. "Me and Matt and Logan. And Scott."

Tag was silent while he processed that. They couldn't know. "Nothing was going on."

Jase laughed. "Riiiiight. You two were just playing Rummikub out there every night."

144

"How'd you know she was there?"

"We saw her a few times between the three of us. One night Logan was coming to see you, and when he heard some noises from inside the tent, he...uh...decided not to bother you. One night Scott went to check on Emily and Kyla's bed was empty. We put it all together. Plus, everyone noticed the way you two were acting."

"*Everyone*?"

"Yeah. Especially Mom."

"Shit."

"So...why are you pissed? Kyla doesn't want to continue the sleepovers now you're back in the city?"

"Neither of us do."

"Really." Jase rubbed his chin. "Why not?"

"Neither of us want a relationship right now. She's too busy with her high-powered law career. Even though it's killing her," he added with a touch of bitterness he couldn't disguise. "And you know why I'm not."

"Jovannah."

"Her and every other woman who just wants to get with a pro athlete."

"Not every woman is like that."

"Okay, *you* found one who's not."

"Yeah." Jase smiled. "Remi wanted nothing to do with me when she found out what I do for a living. Of course, I felt the same about her." He made a face. "She's not into money or status at all."

"Women like Remi are rare."

"Oh yeah." Jase's heartfelt agreement both annoyed Tag and made him envious. "She's pretty special, all right. But I don't know that it's that rare. I mean, the real women are out there. Somewhere. I believe it. That's pretty damn cynical to think all women are like that."

"Well, I haven't seen it."

"So you're saying the reason Kyla slept with you last week was because you're an NHL player?"

"No! *She's* not like that."

"You do know that you're not making a lot of sense, right?"

"Fuck off." Tag's fingers tightened on the steering wheel and his jaw clenched.

"Seriously, man. You can't say all women are like that in one breath and in the next say Kyla's not. So what was it last week, then?"

"It was just…sex."

"Well, nothing wrong with that." Jase nodded. "Sex is good. And you always did have a thing for her."

"I did not."

Jase's laugh grated on his nerves. "You're in bad shape, dude. Look, deal with it. If you want to see her again, call her."

Tag could think of a lot of reasons why he couldn't do that. They'd agreed, no relationship. She was too busy with her quest for partner. He was too busy with his career. They couldn't risk the friendships between all their family members on something that could go horribly wrong. And…probably the biggest…he was terrified of being rejected by her. No way was he confessing that fear to his little brother.

His little brother, who seemed to have grown up a lot lately.

"There's nothing to deal with."

"Okay. Whatever. I tried. Just don't take out your frustrations on the rest of us, okay?"

Tag turned the music back up. They were into the city now, cruising along Portage Avenue, another gorgeous summer day. Hopefully the weather would hold for the tournament. It would be a major pain in the ass if they got rained out.

He sighed. Jase was right. He'd been pissy all week, with everyone. And it was nobody's fault but his. Since he and Kyla had parted at the lake, his mood had dropped like a puck at face off. He couldn't stop thinking about her, which was driving him crazy.

She's not like that.

Okay, so fine. She wasn't the type to use him. She remained

unfazed by his success, unimpressed by his money, oblivious to his celebrity. Yeah, she was obviously happy for him, the way she was happy for Jase and Matt and Logan, the way she celebrated their successes like she did her own brothers'. Clearly her feelings for him weren't brotherly, thank Christ. But he knew she wasn't one of those women who just wanted to sleep with him so she could say she had. He knew she wasn't looking for a rich and famous husband. If there was any woman in the world he trusted, it was Kyla. But all that didn't mean there was anything more to what had happened last week than just some fun.

Except...

He flicked on the blinker and changed lanes to turn onto the Charleswood Bridge.

Except something more *had* happened. He was falling in love with her.

What was he going to do about that? They lived in the same damn city now. Chances were pretty good they were going to run into each other. He could deal with that. But suddenly his single, no-strings-attached life seemed pretty dismal. Especially after seeing what Jase had with Remi. Especially after being with Kyla, so much fun, so undaunted, so unimpressed, but...so admiring, respectful and...loving.

"That's the third time you've let out a big heavy sigh," Jase said. "For Chrissake, go talk to her."

Tag took in a deep breath. Yeah. Maybe he was going to have to do that.

CHAPTER 15

By the end of the week, Kyla had done a lot more thinking about her career. She still hadn't made a decision, but she found herself on-line looking at employment websites, perusing jobs in the legal field. Her mind was starting to open to the idea that maybe she needed to explore other options. She'd left the office at five o'clock every day, had dinner with a couple of girlfriends she hadn't seen for a long time and had laced up her running shoes and gone for a run along the river walk at the Forks.

Today, Friday, was the Heller brothers' charity golf tournament, which she'd signed up for a long time ago. Seeing Tag again made her both nervous and excited.

So she'd never gotten over that little crush on Tag Heller. Sleeping with him had probably been a mistake because she'd gone all female and gotten emotionally involved. Why that hadn't happened with other guys she'd slept with, she wasn't sure, but in any case, she would be in control and friendly and polite when she next saw him.

The golf tournament wasn't fun. She hated doing things she wasn't good at, and despite a lot of expensive golf lessons, hours at the driving range, and a lot of business tournaments, she wasn't exactly a great golfer. She was decent at best, at least not humiliatingly awful, but it wasn't fun for her. She put on a good face, though, especially when she ended up in a foursome with one of the new owners of the Jets, Mike Glendower. Tag's boss.

"So, congratulations on finally making that deal to buy the team," she said with a smile as they prepared to tee off. "You must be so happy."

"Yeah, we're pretty pumped. Thanks."

They discussed some of the complicated business and legal issues that had dragged on for months, the frustrations, the delays. "I'm a lawyer," she explained to Mike, seeing the look of surprise on his face.

"Yeah," he said slowly. "I think I knew that. You're Greg MacIntosh's daughter, aren't you?"

"That's right."

"You're a lawyer at Ingram Howell Grant."

"Yes." She blinked. "I am."

"Ted Ingram is a good friend of mine."

Of course he was.

"I've heard good things about you," Mike added.

"Really." She smiled. "Thanks. That's nice to know."

They next chatted at the second hole as they waited for their companions to tee off.

"You've done a lot of work for the AHL," Mike said. "I remember talking to Craig about that. Craig Pearson."

Craig was the other owner of the team, and yes, he'd been involved with the city's AHL team, and yes, she'd worked with him. "Yes. You *have* heard a lot about me."

"Craig was impressed with you."

"Thank you." She smiled. "That's good to hear."

"You know," Mike said. "We're rebuilding our team here, the off ice team as well. We're looking for new legal counsel."

"Really." What was he saying?

"You're probably not looking for a change, but if you're interested in talking about employment with the Jets, I'd love to talk to you more about it."

She didn't answer, thoughts running wildly through her head. She'd been thinking so much about her career this week, especially after talking to Tag. Especially after that week at the lake where she'd realized how her work was making her literally sick. The firm hadn't made the decision on partner yet. She'd probably get it. But Tag had asked her the question and she was now asking it of herself—was that what she really wanted?

"That's interesting," she said slowly. "Very interesting." She was fascinated by pro sports. She loved hockey.

"Great! Here's my card. Call me at my office Monday morning and we'll set up a meeting next week. No pressure," he added with a sincere smile. "I'm sure you have a lot of questions too. I'll introduce you to some of the other personnel and we'll just have a chat."

"That sounds great."

After eighteen holes, she chatted with other people she knew there, a few clients, people she'd gone to school with. Then she spotted Tag across the lawn, standing near the clubhouse entrance, surrounded by three gorgeous girls smiling up at him. She stood there and watched him for a moment as he talked and laughed, his wide smile flashing charm all over the place, and her heart turned over in her chest. She began walking toward him.

She felt as though her heart reached out to him and he seemed to sense it. He looked up and spotted her. He kept talking, but he didn't take his eyes off her. As she neared the group, he said "Excuse me, ladies," with another charming smile, and detached himself from them. He moved toward her, his gaze still fastened on her face, making her heart tremble and her skin tingle.

"Hi," she said when they stood face to face, a little breathless.

"Hi."

They stared at each other.

"Um," she began. "I was just talking to Mike Glendower."

"Oh yeah?"

"Mmm. He um…wants to talk to me about a job."

Tag lifted one eyebrow. "A job?"

"Legal counsel. He says they're looking for someone here."

Tag's slow smile had her pulse fluttering. "Huh. That's true."

"I just wanted to mention it to you...I don't know what's going to happen. I'm not even sure I'm interested. Although it is intriguing. And I've been thinking a lot about my career this week. Thanks to you."

His lips quirked.

"Would it be a problem for you if I worked for the team? Because I don't want to make things uncomfortable, and if it would be, I won't even call him to set up the meeting."

He didn't answer. His eyes roved over her face. Her heart beat even faster, but she kept a cool smile on her face, her hands steady on the tote bag she held over her shoulder.

"It wouldn't be a problem for me," he said finally, his voice low and smoky. "If it's something you're interested in, go for it."

"It might be."

He moved a little closer. "Kyla..."

She tipped her head back to look up at him, so tall, so broad, so handsome.

"I missed you this week," he said quietly.

Everything inside her melted into liquid. Her mouth went soft and her eyes closed briefly at the surge of emotion inside her. "Oh." She looked at him again, saw her own feelings reflected back in his brown eyes. "I missed you too."

"Tag Heller!" A man stopped beside them. Kyla didn't know him, but Tag did.

"Hey, Norm. How are you?"

"Great! Just wanted to say hi and tell you how happy we all are the team's back in town."

"Thanks." Tag's smile held charm and enthusiasm. "Glad to be here. It's going to be an exciting year."

"Yeah, definitely." The man glanced at Kyla.

Tag introduced them and Kyla shook hands and smiled.

"Great turnout this year," Norm said.

"Definitely." Tag grinned. "The team moving back brought a lot of attention to our little golf tournament. I think we raised a good chunk of cash for Children's Hospital today."

"Sure hope so, it's a good cause. Nice to see you again. Good luck this season."

"Thanks."

And Norm moved on.

"I wish we could get out of here." Tag slid his hand around her arm. "But I have to stick around for a while."

"I know."

Their eyes met and held again in a connection of heat and longing. "I know what we said," he murmured, his face so close to hers she could see the glint of whiskers on his jaw, the flecks of gold and cinnamon in his eyes. She could breathe in his scent, that fresh clean scent. "Up at the lake. How neither of us was looking for a relationship."

She nodded, holding his gaze.

"I wasn't looking for one." He touched her cheek, fingertips grazing her jaw. "But I think it found me."

A tremulous smile tugged at her lips. "Oh yeah?"

He bent and touched his nose to hers. "Yeah."

"Well, I wasn't looking for one either. Didn't have time. But this week…I seem to have freed up some time in my life for other things. Thanks to a very smart man who annoyed me with some tough questions."

He smiled. "That's good." He paused. "I've been burnt a few times, Kyla. I kind of have a hard time trusting women."

"Me?" Her stomach tightened.

"No. Not you. *Never* you. That's why…I—"

"Jesus." Someone slapped Tag on the back and Kyla looked up to see Logan standing there grinning. "Would you two get a room?"

Heat scorched her cheeks, but she smiled back at Logan. His grin held warm affection.

"Shaddup," Tag said mildly. His hand slid down Kyla's bare arm until it clasped her hand in a warm grip.

"Or should I say a tent," Logan added with a wicked little lift of one eyebrow that reminded her of Tag.

"Uh…" Bereft of words, she looked at Tag, who was grinning broadly. He shrugged as he met her eyes. Logan moved away to talk to someone else.

"I said nothing," he murmured in her ear. "I can't help it if people noticed things."

"Like your mother." She bit her lip. "Tag…"

"I know. I'm not taking this lightly, Kyla." He regarded her seriously, turning to face her, holding both her hands with his. Once again, he seemed to know what she was thinking.

"Your mom talked to me. Up at the lake. I felt horrible because she thought there was something between us and she was all happy about it. I had to tell her it wasn't really anything. If we mess this up…"

"I know. I hear you. I'm picking up what you're putting down." She laughed reluctantly. "Seriously, Tag."

"I am serious. As serious as a game misconduct. No, as serious as a full season suspension. I know what this means. I know the consequences of things going wrong, believe me. But Kyla…I need you." He paused and she saw the vulnerability in his eyes, the same as she felt. "I never thought I'd say this. I want a relationship. It's true, I wasn't looking for one, but…well, I want one with you."

The vulnerability she saw somehow reassured her and made her want to reassure him. "Oh, me too," she said in a rush. "I never realized what it would be like…"

They were both dancing around it, like two players squaring off for a fight, both knowing it was too soon to be talking about love and forever, but knowing they both felt it.

"This isn't the place to be talking about this stuff," she whispered.

"Kyla."

"What?"

"Wanna go on a date with me?"

A bubble of joy rose up inside her and made her laugh. "A date?"

"Yeah. You know. Like a couple. Maybe dinner. I know this really cool place on Portage, across from Assiniboine Park. Tiny little place, great food. Tomorrow night."

She lowered her eyelashes, breathed in the smell of him, absorbed the warmth of his body. "Oh. A date." She smiled and tipped her head back. "I'd like that. But just so you know...I don't put out on the first date."

He laughed and brushed his mouth over hers. "We'll see about that."

Tag arrived at Kyla's downtown condo at seven-thirty Saturday night. She let him in and he took in her appearance. The shorts, flip flops and pony tail from the lake had been replaced with a tight little black dress, long glossy hair and shiny lips...and heels.

"Christ, you're gorgeous." His gaze tracked back up those amazing legs, the hem of the dress a few inches above her knees, then over the curves the snug dress outlined.

"Thank you. You look good too."

He shrugged and she laughed, laying a palm on his cheek. "You *are* gorgeous." She went up on her toes to kiss his jaw. "Mmm. And you smell good too." She breathed in. "Really good."

He clasped her hips. "That's good. Because if you thought I stink, that would not bode well for us."

She smiled up at him. "True."

"Having said that, there are plenty of times I do stink." He grimaced. "And you know how bad hockey equipment can smell."

"I know. I remember driving home from one of Scott's games almost gagging the whole way. He thought I was doing it just to yank his chain, but honestly...it was rank." She stepped back and moved into the condo. "Come on in. So this is my place."

154

"I like it." He looked around as he strolled in, taking in the exposed ductwork, the gorgeous old brick on the outside wall and arched windows. The space wasn't large, but had a warm homey feel with thick rugs on hardwood floors, a small lamp on a low table next to the couch and comfortable-looking leather furniture.

"Thanks. It's close to work."

"You like living downtown?"

She picked up her purse. "It's different. I like it for now. But you know...some day it would be nice to have a yard. I'd like to try growing things."

"You'd need spare time to spend in a yard."

She grinned. "I felt that dig."

They left her condo and rode the elevator down to the lobby. Out on the street, the summer evening was still warm. Trees lined the street in front of old turn-of-the-century buildings, former warehouses that now housed condominiums like Kyla's, offices and restaurants.

He'd parked a half block away, and she tapped along a cobblestone sidewalk beside him. He eyed the heels, but she seemed used to navigating in them. He paused next to his Jeep. "Here we go." He opened the door for her and helped her in.

"New vehicle?"

"Yep." He rounded the front and slid in. "You like?"

"It's really big."

He smiled. "That's what she said." He gave her an arched eyebrow.

She burst out laughing. "Oh quit bragging. You don't have to convince me."

He laughed too and pulled away from the curb. "I guess we could've gone somewhere downtown."

"This is fine. Where are we going?"

"Maison Blanche. It's in a big old house near Assiniboine Park."

"I've heard of it, but I haven't been there. Let me guess...it's a white house."

155

His lips twitched. "Yes, it is."

It wasn't a long drive and soon they were seated in a cozy booth at the very back of the restaurant. He'd totally used who he was when he made the reservation, asking for the back booth so few people would see them. It was a tiny place, but still...

"Can I have your autograph?"

They hadn't even opened their menus before the first request came. "Sure." Tag smiled and scrawled his signature. Other people in the full restaurant were eying him, but most respected his privacy.

"Those girls are giving me the evil eye," Kyla whispered.

"What girls?"

"The ones at the table over there." She lifted her chin, her menu open in front of her face. "They're actually pissed off that you're here with a girl!"

"See how lucky you are?"

She met his eyes and shook her head, lips pursed. "You conceited ass."

He leaned across the table. "You know I'm not."

"I know."

"The fact that you're all mystified by why they're jealous would take my ego down a notch if I was."

Her smile glowed. "I know exactly why they're jealous." She leaned forward too so their faces were only inches apart. "And they should be."

His chest warmed. Fuck, he was crazy about this woman.

They ordered mussels to share and a bottle of wine. Kyla ordered a grilled chicken breast with tomato jam that sounded interesting, and Tag requested the beef bourguignon.

"Want to come look at some houses with me tomorrow?" Tag swirled the red wine in his glass.

"Houses? Like, to buy?"

"Yeah. I have to find a place to live. Staying with my parents might make me nuts."

"Your parents are awesome."

"Yeah, I know. But a week of all that family time was enough. I need out of there."

"And here I was all crying my eyes out when I left the lake last weekend because I was going to miss everyone so much."

"Big tough lawyer's not so tough."

"Apparently not." One corner of her mouth lifted. "I was all resistant to going up there for the week and then I cried when I had to leave. It was a great week."

"In many ways."

Their eyes met with a little burst of heat and sparks.

"Where are you looking?"

"Huh?" He frowned.

"For houses."

"Oh. Yeah. Tuxedo. Same as Mom and Dad."

"And yet you want to get away from them." She smirked as she lifted her wine glass to her lips.

"Ha. Okay, not that far. Hey, it's a nice neighborhood."

"Something on Wellington Crescent perhaps?" She named the street that probably had the highest-priced houses in town.

"Nah. It's not a status thing. I just like older neighborhoods, with lots of trees...and I may as well be close to them. Mom's a pretty good cook."

Kyla laughed.

"How was work this week? They survived without you?"

"Yes, they did." She rolled her eyes. "As we both knew they would."

"No word on partner?"

"Nope." She paused. "You should be proud of me. I went for a run this week. I left the office at five o'clock every day, and only answered a couple of emails in the evenings."

He smiled.

"And I had dinner with some girlfriends I haven't seen for a while."

"Good for you."

"Yeah. It was fun."

"Are you seriously thinking about taking another job?"

She bit her lip. "I'm not sure. I did some looking around last week. That conversation with Mike Glendower came out of nowhere." Her eyebrows pulled together. "I'm not sure that working for a hockey team would be any less of an old boy's club than Ingram Howell Grant."

Tag considered that. "Yeah, I don't know either. There weren't many women in team management in Phoenix. But they're putting together a new team here, so it might be different."

"It's something to think about."

Tag looked down at his wine. "I like talking to you, Kyla."

"Thank you." Her voice was soft, and he lifted his head to meet her eyes. "I like talking to you too."

He leaned closer again and lowered his voice. "Of course, I also like fucking you."

Her cheeks flamed bright red and her eyelids lowered. "Tag!"

"Seriously. That exquisite body needs to be fucked hard. I also like spanking that tight little ass."

Her cheeks got even redder.

"Nobody can hear us." He glanced around the room. They could barely hear the music playing, the muted roar of voices talking in the room was so loud.

She looked up at him through her eyelashes.

"You like it when I talk dirty, don't you, you hot, sexy girl. Can't wait to have you in my bed tonight again."

"I told you I don't put out on the first date."

"And you know I love a challenge."

Her little chin lifted. "And so do I."

"It's on, then. Bring it. We'll see whether we end up in bed."

They shared a heated smile.

CHAPTER 16

They ended up in bed.

Kyla didn't really try that hard to resist. Yes, she liked a challenge. Yes, she liked to win. But damn, this didn't feel like losing… it felt too damn good.

"I win," Tag breathed in her ear, when he had her naked in her bed.

"No, you don't."

His head shot up and he laughed out loud. "Say what?"

Her mind worked. She could argue about anything…when her brain cells weren't being fried with lust… "You said you couldn't wait to get me in *your* bed," she finally panted as he ran his tongue over her collarbone. "This isn't your bed. This is *my* bed. Therefore I win."

He rolled off her and collapsed onto his back laughing. "Jesus Christ."

She moved over him, smiling. "You can't deny that."

He laughed more. "No, you're right."

"You weren't planning to take me back to your parents' place tonight, obviously."

"Obviously." His hand landed on her butt in a sweetly stinging spank. "You sexy little smartass. You know I never really meant we were going to end up literally in *my* bed."

"That's what you said." She tilted her head challengingly.

He spanked her again and a moan leaked from her lips. She buried her face in the side of his neck as the skin of her ass warmed and liquid heat gathered between her thighs.

He rolled her again so she was on her back, pressing her down into the mattress with a dominance that thrilled her, yet with a gentleness that moved her. "You might make me crazy."

"I hope so."

He cupped her breasts, stared at them reverently, then lowered his head to kiss and lick and suck them. He tugged her nipples with his mouth until they became hot points of pleasure. Sensations shimmered over her body, pinpricks of pleasure racing over her. A desperate aching need built between her legs.

"You need to come, don't you beautiful girl." He slipped a hand between her thighs. She parted them eagerly for him, lifting into his palm. "Oh yeah. So hot and wet, baby." Then he gave her a little spank there, right on her pussy. Heat shot through her in an ecstatic burst of pleasure.

She felt drunk, not just from the wine she'd had at dinner, but from all the sensations…Tag's hands on her, his mouth on her, his big hot body pressed against her. Dizzy and breathless, her body soft and wet and pulsing, she needed more. She needed everything…all of him.

"Please. Inside me. I need you."

"Fuck yeah."

He already had a condom on. He entered her and her body surrounded him, accepted him. She lifted her knees and hooked her ankles at the small of his back, urging him deeper. And deeper.

His body inside her felt right. Perfect. Complete. They fit together, they moved together in an intimate rhythm. Their soft sighs and the sounds of their slick bodies moving together filled her bedroom.

He took her higher, sliding a hand between them to find her clit, finding the exact place, rubbing with a sure and perfect touch. Inside her, he thrust deep, filling her almost to the point of pain, a sharp sweet ecstasy. Everything drew up inside her tighter, higher. She hovered there, wanting to come, awash with almost unbearable sensation. She cried out and clutched his shoulders, and still it went on and on...and then it burst and shattered. She shuddered, clinging to him with her hands, her teeth sinking into his shoulder.

They pressed through their orgasms together, long, blinding, wrenching spasms, until they lay wrapped around each other in perfect intimacy and wild rapture. She pressed her mouth to his shoulder.

"Tag," she whispered, arms and legs tight around him. "Tag."

"Yeah, baby. I know." He lifted his head. "I love you, Kyla."

"I love you too." Tears flooded her eyes. "I always have."

His face softened. "I kinda think I always loved you too. It just took us a helluva long time to figure it out."

"I missed you so much this week."

"Me too." He kissed her nose. "My bed was cold and empty without you."

"Yes, exactly." She gave a shaky sigh. "I'm so glad you're here now."

"Fuck, so am I. So am I." He kissed her mouth before moving off her, slowly withdrawing. He disappeared into the bathroom for a minute, then slid back in with her, reaching for her.

She curled up against him. It was crazy. She hadn't wanted a relationship. The idea of a man pressuring her for time that she didn't have made her insides twist up in knots. But Tag...she'd give him anything he wanted. Whatever she had to give, she would do it. Okay, okay, she wasn't going to sacrifice her entire career for him. But maybe now she had something...someone...who was worth giving things up for.

And somehow she didn't think she'd feel like she was losing anything. She'd be getting so much in return. A man who loved her

161

and cared about her too, who wanted the best for her the way she did for him.

If she made partner, great. But it would be on her terms. And if she didn't make partner…she'd figure out what she wanted to do with her life. And she'd do it with this man.

"Where are you off to?"

Tag set the jug of milk back in the fridge and glanced at his mom. "Going to look at houses."

"Oh thank god."

He lifted an eyebrow. "You want to get rid of me?"

She laughed. "I'm kidding. You can stay here as long as you want. I think you'd rather be on your own, though." She paused. "You didn't come home last night."

"Nope." Okay. He drew in a long breath. Here it was. "I was with Kyla last night."

"Oh." Mom blinked. Then her eyes widened. "Ooooh."

"Yeah."

Her eyes went wide again. "You and Kyla…?"

"Yeah."

"Oh praise the sweet baby Jesus."

He grinned. "She told me she thought you were kind of hoping for this."

"It's taken you long enough, for heaven's sake!"

"Mom. Seriously…you're okay with it?"

"Yes!" She looked like she was about to leap up onto the island and do the Riverdance. "Oh my god, yes! You know I love that girl."

"I know. I do. But…" His gut torqued. "What if…what if things don't work out? What about your friendship with Jenn and Greg?"

Mom bit her lip. "Things will work out."

"But what if they don't?"

"Taggart Heller, you better not be just messing around with that sweet girl." She gave him a terrifying scowl.

He held his hands up. "I'm not, I swear I'm not. I love her, Mom."

"Oh." She sniffled.

"I want things to work out. But we're both a little...concerned about the family thing."

Mom swallowed and nodded. "Okay, I get that. But we're all adults and if, god forbid, something happens...we'll deal with it." She narrowed her eyes at him. "But if you screw around on her or break her heart, I will hurt you. Don't think I can't, just because you're a hundred pounds heavier than me now."

"A hundred pounds. Phhhht."

Her gaze grew frostier. "How much do you think I weigh?"

"Er...yeah, a hundred pounds sounds about right, actually."

She grinned. "Tag. I'm so happy for you both. Invite her for dinner tonight."

"Jesus, we just spent a whole week together at the lake."

To his surprise, Mom laughed. "True. You two probably want some alone time. That's fine."

"She's coming with me to look at houses this afternoon."

Mom sighed. "That's wonderful."

Dad walked into the kitchen. "What's going on?"

"Tag and Kyla are together!" Mom nearly bounced.

Dad gave him a long, slow look. "Uh huh." He adjusted his glasses on his nose. "Glad you're finally being out in the open about it instead of sneaking around. Sleeping in a ten. Fishing. Ha. Is there any more coffee?"

Tag grinned. Okay. His parents' reaction was cool. Hopefully the MacIntoshes would be similar. Kyla was across the street now, talking to her parents.

"I dropped Kyla off at her folks' place. Heading over there now to get her. Let's hope they're as happy as you are."

163

He crossed the street, tossing his keys in his hand. They were meeting the realtor at the first house at one o'clock. He rang the front doorbell, then opened the door and poked his head in.

Kyla appeared in the long center hall. "Hi."

His heart expanded at seeing her. *His*. She was his. "Hi." He stepped in and closed the door behind him.

Jenn walked up behind Kyla. "Tag." She smiled. "Come on in."

He slid his arm around Kyla's waist. Well, Jenn didn't have a shot gun aimed at him, so that was good. Not that the MacIntoshes even owned a shot gun.

"Okay?" he murmured in Kyla's ear.

She nodded, and slanted a smile up at him. "Yeah. But I got quite a lecture."

"Huh?"

Kyla's dad showed up then too. "We just told her that a relationship involves give and take. And if one person spends all their time working, they're not giving much to the relationship."

"I get it, Dad," Kyla said. "I already figured that out. Don't worry."

Tag grinned. He reached out and shook Greg's hand. "I'll keep reminding her of that."

"You do that." Greg gripped his hand in a firm clasp and smiled.

They chatted with Jenn and Gregg for a few minutes, then headed out to view the first house, only about five blocks away.

"Well that's a relief," Kyla said in the Jeep. "Although my parents apparently don't think much of me if they think I'd abandon you for my job."

"I trust you won't do that, babe. And hey, my mom's worried about me screwing around on you."

"What?"

"You trust me too right?" He looked into her eyes. "You know I wouldn't do that?"

"You better not!" Her face softened. "I trust you, Tag. You're a good man."

164

Her faith in him made him want to be that man—good and honorable and faithful. "Thank you."

Tag entered Kyla's condo with the key she'd given him weeks ago. He'd just come from an intense workout. Physicals and training camp were only a few weeks away now. He needed to be in shape. At thirty-one, he was competing against young guys trying to break into the NHL and he wasn't giving anyone a chance to push him out.

The idea of retirement floated through his head, as it had off and on over the last year. He didn't want to retire now. With the team back in Winnipeg, playing in front of this kind of fan base was going to be amazing. The team was making changes, rebuilding, and he wanted to be part of that. Realistically, a Stanley Cup was a few years away and he might never have that. That kind of saddened him, truth be told, but he'd had a great career.

But maybe he needed to start thinking about what he'd do after hockey. Or, after *playing* hockey. He'd still like to be involved in the sport in some capacity. Maybe there was a way he could help the team continue to improve and build even after he was done playing.

"You're home!"

He started. He hadn't expected Kyla to be home at four in the afternoon on a Friday. "Jesus, babe, you scared me. What are you doing here?"

She grinned. "I left work early."

"I see that." He frowned. "Are you sick?"

"No! I can take off early on a Friday without being sick. Actually…I came home to celebrate."

He paused. Was she talking about… "Did they make their decision about partner?"

"Yes!" She actually jumped up and down. "I got it!"

"Oh baby, that's fucking fantastic. C'mere."

She flew into his arms for a fierce hug.

Something huge and hot expanded in his chest as he squeezed her. "Congratulations. So happy for you."

"Thank you." She drew back. "You would have been proud of me, though. I told them I would work hard and bring in business… but I was also going to have work-life balance. And if they couldn't accept that, I would turn down the partnership and let someone else have the opportunity. It didn't hurt that somehow Ted Ingram got word that I had talked to Mike Glendower." She made a face. "I never used that and I wouldn't use my connections to the team to get this, but…it might have helped."

He kissed her forehead. "You go right ahead and use me, baby."

She laughed.

"So they went for that?"

"They apparently want to keep me." She smiled.

"Of course they do. And you're sure this is what you want?"

She sighed. "I went on those interviews, and I talked to Mike, but…yeah. This is what I want. And I feel better knowing that if it really doesn't work out, I have other options."

"Sure you do. Because you're amazing."

"I love you."

He smooched her lips. "Love you too. Congratulations again."

"So, I picked up a bottle of champagne for us to celebrate tonight."

"That's one way to celebrate." He swooped and picked her up in his arms.

"Tag!"

"Here's another." He carried her down the hall to her bedroom where he proceeded to congratulate her very thoroughly.

Thank you so much for reading Faceoff! Make sure you're on my mailing list for news about my next releases. If you enjoyed Face-

166

off, please consider leaving a review at the retailer of your choice or at Goodreads to help other readers find my books. You can also contact me at info@kellyjamieson.com to tell me what you thought of it or ask me any questions!

And enjoy this sneak peek at Heller Brothers Hockey Book 3

OTHER BOOKS BY KELLY JAMIESON

Heller Brothers Hockey

Breakaway

Faceoff

One Man Advantage

Hat Trick

Offside

Power Series

Rule of Three Series

San Amaro Singles

Windy City Kink

Brew Crew

Aces Hockey

Last Shot

Bayard Hockey

Stand-Alone Books

Dancing in the Rain

Three of Hearts

Loving Maddie from A to Z

Love Me

Friends with Benefits

Love Me More

2 Hot 2 Handle

Lost and Found

One Wicked Night

Sweet Deal

Hot Ride

Crazy Ever After

All I Want for Christmas

Sexpresso Night

Irish Sex Fairy

Conference Call

Rigger

You Really Got Me

How Sweet It Is

ABOUT THE AUTHOR

Kelly Jamieson is the bestselling author of over thirty romance novels and novellas. Her writing has been described as "emotionally complex", "sweet and satisfying" and "blisteringly sexy". If she can stop herself from reading or writing, she loves to cook. She has shelves of cookbooks that she reads at length. She also enjoys gardening in the summer, and in the winter she likes to read gardening magazines and seed catalogues (there might be a theme here...) She also loves shopping, especially for clothes and shoes.

Subscribe to her newsletter for updates about her new books and what's coming up.

Find out what's new...
www.kellyjamieson.com
info@kellyjamieson.com

www.ingramcontent.com/pod-product-compliance
Lightning Source LLC
Chambersburg PA
CBHW051823170626
46807CB00003B/995